<u>Also by Joseph John Lee</u>

<u>The Spellbinders and the Gunslingers</u>
The Bleeding Stone
The Children of the Black Moon
The Legion of the Lost

<u>Novellas</u>
Pale Night, Red Fields

Upscaled

The Dragons of Nóra, Book One
Joseph John Lee

Eclipseborn Publishing

For Alice and Cam.

If you do ever end up finding a dragon in real life, let me know.

Prologue

G enerations ago, the Inquisition of the Priory of the Thrice-Dead Prophet decided two things: one, that their name was too long; and two, that dragons were a great evil upon the land of Nóra and needed to be vanquished. Their preoccupation with the latter precluded them from addressing the former.

In ages past, dragons were considered the caretakers of Nóra, guardians to whom reverence was paid in return for blessings in the form of bountiful harvests and troves of wisdom. Verdant green land marked the ground they touched, and pristine blue skies graced the air through which they soared, and so long as that remained true, none would think of them as anything other than benevolent.

However, the Inquisition, ever vigilant in its pursuit of anything that could be interpreted as a snake (though the interpretation was, at best, loose) set upon the dragons with ferocity until the guardians that once blessed and protected Nóra faded to legend, becoming bedtime stories used to frighten children.

Though the Inquisition was steadfast in destroying any and all accounts of the harvests, health, and other blessings granted upon Nóra by the dragons, it was inevitable that inquisitive minds would seek out the truths that could evade the Inquisition's swords, torches, and stern talking-tos over the decades and centuries to come. It was also inevitable that these minds would go into hiding to also evade those aforementioned swords, torches, and stern talking-tos, though it was the inclination of some to view exile not as a punishment, but simply as an opportunity to read in peace and quiet.

Try as they might, the Inquisition could not rid Nóra of *all* the dragons, and those who survived fled to the northern reaches past the three Cliffs of Ard—the Tall Cliffs, the Small Cliffs, and the Awaiting-a-Growth-Spurt Cliffs—in a region known as the Draconic Highlands. Per the Inquisition's teachings, this location is both forbidden and a paradox, because it forces them to admit they did not slay *all* the dragons, and they were much too prideful for that.

Within that paradox rests the crux of the matter: the truth. An inquisitive mind would find their truth where they would, but whether it was *the* truth was a different matter. Anything written contrary to the Inquisition's narrow view was deemed forbidden, but a curious mind should always be intrigued by that which has been prohibited. Legends bred intrigue, and intrigue bred rumors, and despite the Inquisition's best efforts, rumors would be heeded by a different sort.

Any forbidden knowledge was game for forbidden trade, and thus, peddlers, traders, poachers, and other general ne'er-do-wells would seek remnants of draconic lore: scales, claws, teeth...and sometimes the rare egg.

And when comes an egg, there may come a hatchling, and there may come a story to tell.

Chapter One

Luckily, there *is* a story to tell.

No, nothing of the sort where a chosen hero embarks upon a quest atop their scaled mount, soaring through the sky to stop a great evil. Remember, the Inquisition banned that sort of thing.

Rather, this is a tale of a simpler kind. One that began in the humble village of Baile, smack in the middle of Nóra, far from the crashing waves of the southern shores and the bustle of the trading ports to the east, but near enough to the ever-present smell of day-old bread, week-old fish, and far-too-old dung (both bovine *and* human).

Against that refreshing air, a wagon crested the northern horizon. Wagons never approached Baile; most merchants worth their salt would go out of their way to *avoid* the village. Nóran traders lived by a creed: "By land, by sea, not by Baile unless dung you wish to see." Only the usual couriers ventured to the village to deliver grains and seafood, but even they were reluctant.

It was those few newcomers who did dare to approach that would become the subject of young Ailís's attention. And this was going to be a great morning.

As she walked out of her house with her ma's instructions for the market in hand, she looked at her brother beside her and pointed northward. "Hey Cam. Take a look."

Camaráin, younger by four years, followed the path of her finger, squinting his dark eyes. He grunted. "Haven't seen anyone new come around here in a while."

Ailís flashed a smile. "Are you thinking what I'm thinking?"

Rolling his eyes, Camaráin planted his hands on his hips and said, "Not again, Ailís. The last time we did that, Ma got real cross with us."

"Then we'll just have to be sneakier about it." She pushed him toward the market, where the well-trodden path marked the perfect spot to set up. "Come on, little brother. I don't want to go to my dancing lessons, and you don't want to do choring. What more could you ask for?"

"Well, you got me there." He smiled, the wind tussling his mop of dark hair. "Let's do it, then."

The perfect spot loomed ahead, right at the clearing where the market opened up and the remnants of wagon wheels and footsteps had sunken in. Already, Ailís could feel her excitement welling. She had to find it where she could in this village.

Baile was quaint in its mundanity. Stalls lined the square of the morning market, peddlers announcing their wares and goods for all to hear until their voices grew hoarse or they were kicked by a horse. (It was known to happen. Nóran horses were temperamental.) The homemakers and home breakers perused the selections or took up space, as was the routine. Pockets of mud collected underfoot after the latest mist of morning rain.

See? Quaint. The villagers of Baile had dug themselves into

their comfortable rut and very little was wont to pull them out of it.

An outlander was typically all that could pull Ailís out of hers. Even if it was but a moment's curiosity, she could not help but stop at the crest of the market, feign some interest in the produce her ma instructed her to purchase, and drag her foot back and forth, back and forth, until a nice, deep divot formed. She certainly couldn't help it if Camaráin did the same beside her, standing at about a wagon's width away, until a deep enough indentation formed that the inattentive eye simply could not see. When Ailís looked down, she had to summon the shock required to see her freshly-cleaned skirt had once again been dirtied by mud, and therefore she'd need to duck behind an empty stall to try and clean it—typically the stall beside the vegetable stand where her ma always told her to purchase fresh produce (strangely, that stand never had fresh enough vegetables, according to Ailís). And it was there that they'd wait.

When the sound of clattering horseshoes approached, she knew it was time to peer around the corner of the stall. Directing the tall horse-driven wagon was a courier she had never seen before, someone who did not smell of fresh seaside catches—or what had been the fresh catch however many days ago. The driver was a young man whose face brimmed with self-importance. Had Ailís not known any better, she'd have thought him to be a prince or lord from one of the stories her uncle used to read to her, his face framed with prominent cheekbones and long, blonde hair that were the image of gallantry. But alas, the illusion was broken the moment the front right wheel of his wagon caught in the divots, sending him plummeting to the ground with a wet thud.

It was difficult to stifle her laughter, but Ailís managed. She glanced at Camaráin, hand over her mouth as amused spittle escaped between the slits of her fingers. It was far from the first time Ailís had entertained herself in such a way, but she had never seen the horses buck as they did, worsened only by the concerned marketgoers crowding around both the fallen merchant and his temperamental steeds.

The horse jolted, prevented from taking off only by the quick thinking of a well-attuned carer, but the rear of the wagon had shifted and was now stuck in the divot, entrenched too deep, and whatever cargo sat within began to jostle and roll and bounce.

Some right out of the carriage. Some rolling past Ailís's vision and stopping around the corner.

Brushing the specks of mud off the hem of her skirt, she looked at Camaráin and inclined her head toward the corner. "Come, little brother, before someone sees us," she said, leaving, "before someone tells Ma again" unspoken.

Camaráin was all too familiar with the tone and was quick to crawl after her. There had been plenty a time when the attempted escape from trouble was ill-planned or ill-executed—on both of their parts. Even now, they would be hard-pressed to avoid chastisement from their ma for the mud already soaking their clothes. Freshly cleaned clothes, at that! But it was preferable to being spotted at the scene of a merchant's damaged wagon.

An oblong shape ceased its rolling some paces down the path behind the storage tents. Ailís hummed to herself, impressed at the size of the object and how it managed not to crack or splinter. Even more impressive was how far it was able to roll in the mud as though it had a mind of its own and was intent on escaping. It wouldn't have been the first time such a thing happened in Baile; the Harvest Festival of four autumns past was still a sore subject amongst the smiths (and the bakers as well, for some reason).

But when Ailís kneeled beside the object, her breath caught. There was a rank stench nearby that was certainly part of the reason, but she was also shocked.

Years ago, when she was wee, younger than Camaráin even, her uncle Iósaf would often regale her with stories of dragons. Not the kind to frighten her into obedience as the Inquisition would have applauded and endorsed, but of a warmer nature, where dragons were not beings of wickedness but rather benevolent creatures such that belonged only to the legends. It had been years since she had last seen her uncle and her ma would not tell her why, but even after all this time, the imagery of Iósaf's tales remained with her. The serpentine forms as they glided through the sky, the blessings upon the earth wherever they traveled...

And the eggs from which the dragons hatched.

Her eyes widened.

"Cam!" Ailís hissed in a sharp whisper, trying and failing to keep her voice down amidst her excitement. "It's...it's..."

Camaráin had already been walking toward her, adjusting the strap on the bag fastened around his chest. "It can't be," he said, equally shocked.

Her hands shaking, Ailís reached out and touched the egg, its scales coarse against her fingertips. A steady vibration hummed at her touch, cool as a gentle breeze and without the potent aromas that often accompanied such breezes in Baile. "But what is a dragon egg doing here?"

"And why did *he* have it?" Camaráin added, gesturing to the merchant still being tended to at the main thoroughfare, judging from the clamor of well-wishes, whinnies, and mocking laughter from that one hawker who always was amused at others' misfortune (it was a wonder he ever sold anything, but people liked wool). "And where did he get it to begin with?"

"I don't know, but..." A smile grew wide on Ailís's face, revealing her canvas of half-grown adult teeth and half-loose baby teeth. "I don't think he's supposed to have it."

"No one is! Dragons aren't supposed to be exist anymore!"

(Again, the paradox of the Inquisition claiming to have slain all the dragons while also admitting their existence beyond the Cliffs of Ard.)

Ailís gestured toward the egg. "And yet, here's proof of one." She opened her messenger bag, empty of the produce she promised she'd purchase and deposited the egg inside. "There's still plenty of things in his wagon. I'm sure he won't miss this."

Camaráin grinned. "We should get home. Before the Inquisitors start asking questions."

The clink and clank of armored steps indicated an Inquisitor or two had already begun doing just that, and fluster of the merchant's answers was all the sign the kids needed to know they had time to get home. Rolling in the mud of a Baile street was a harrowing experience for the uninitiated.

Keeping her laughter to herself, Ailís scurried along the back of the market with her brother in tow until at last reemerging into the main throughfare, where the fallen merchant's wagon had lain fresh trails in the mud. Home was just ahead, at the end of the line of identical houses, all crafted from the same carpenter's hands and probably supplied by the same tree.

Theirs was the one likely carved from the stump or by the carpenter's handless apprentice. It was a floor shorter and still looked half-finished after all these years, but at least they'd never got lost on the way home. Their ma always said, "It has character."

Ailís opened the door and was welcomed by the aroma of fresh soda bread, a much-needed reprieve from the odor of the markets. The loaf sat on the dining table at the edge of the room by the window, and she could not help but be drawn to it. She licked her lips and tapped her fingertips together, looking over both shoulders to ensure the coast was clear before reaching for the nearby knife. The blade slid against the wooden table, cutting a swath through the air as Ailís held it high, and—

"Ah-ah-ah!" a voice called from the other room.

Ailís groaned and dropped the knife, the metal clattering on the table and nearly falling to the floor. "How do you always know?" she asked, craning her head to her right.

Ma emerged from around the corner, drying her hands with a flour-stained towel. Her dark brown hair was tied in a messy bun, allowing the spots of dough to show on her round face. Tossing the towel over her shoulder, she walked to the other side of the room, doing little to acknowledge Ailís and Camaráin beyond a brief smile. "It wouldn't be the first time you thought 'being sneaky' meant 'loudly shuffling your feet along the floor,'" she said with tired eyes. "Only this time, I've learned not to fall for the, 'But, Ma, the loaf was *always* this small!'"

"I told you she wouldn't believe you," Camaráin whispered beneath his breath, rushing off to his bedroom and quickly taking his bag off his shoulders.

Ailís repeated her brother's words with a mocking tone, scrunching her face and sticking out her tongue as she watched him walk by.

Ignoring the children's banter—or perhaps too exhausted to acknowledge it—Ma turned back to the counter and began laying down more flour. "Did you get the eggs from the market like I asked?"

Ailís's initial instinct was to say, "I got *an* egg," but she thought against it, knowing not only would Ma not appreciate the ambiguity, it also would be ill-advised to state that she only procured *one* egg. Instead, she remained silent and flashed her teeth in what passed for a smile.

With an exasperated sigh, Ma turned and looked at her daughter with annoyance. "Ailís, what were you doing at the market for so long? You brought nothing home, you're late for dance, and—" She gasped, as though finally looking at the mud speckling the hem of Ailís's skirt. Shaking her head, she gestured her daughter in the direction of her bedroom. "We'll talk about this later. Go get changed. You needed to be ready for your dance lessons half an hour ago."

"Yes, Ma." Ailís hung her head low, making a great show of it even though she did not feel quite as despondent as she should have been. Her bag bounced against her hip as she walked and she tucked it closely to her chest.

Raising an eyebrow, Ma crossed her arms as Ailís walked by.

"What are you hiding?"

Ailís didn't stop walking. "Nothing," she said, a hint of anxiety coloring her voice.

"Ailís."

"Nothing," she repeated.

"Stop, Ailís," Ma said, taking long steps after her daughter and reaching for the bag strap.

"I said, there's nothing!" Ailís cried as she was spun around, her arms pressing against the top of the egg, pushing it down. The canvas's threads began to fray and tear as she continued to grasp her bag, not at all selling her assertion that she had nothing to hide.

It was only when the bag tore open and its contents hit the floor with a thud that it was apparent that said assertion was, in fact, a bit of a crock.

Ailís's eyes remained on the egg for too long. When she looked up, Ma's eyes were equal parts anger and confusion. All Ailís could think to do was hold up her torn bag and say, "See! There's nothing in here!"

A deep frown stretched across Ma's face. "Ailís," she said calmly, almost alarmingly so. "What is this?" She gestured to the floor.

Creaking footsteps from behind indicated Camaráin emerged from his room and stood in Ailís's periphery in silence.

"Well," Ailís said, allowing the empty canvas bag to fall back to her hip. "I got *an* egg."

Ma hardly appeared in the mood for jokes, but before any words of admonishment could be unleashed, a sound drew both their attention.

A cracking. Not of the floor...but of the egg. Not from the point of impact...but from the top of it.

Ailís kneeled beside it, her eyes glimmering with astonishment. "It's...it's..."

The oblong shape of the egg teetered back and forth, a shard breaking loose in a startling crack, followed by another, and then another. A small silver-scaled leg reached through the opening, talons clutching the edge. A meek chirp sounded within as a second leg took hold and toppled the egg over. A serpentine face peered out, its head no larger than that of a housecat.

Her breath catching in her chest, Ailís could hardly believe what she was seeing.

Dragons had returned to the land of Nóra. Score one against the Inquisition.

Chapter Two

"It's...a...*DRAgnhnhn!*"

As much as Ailís wanted to voice her excitement for the hatchling DRAgnhnhn crawling out of the cracking egg, it would have been a poor decision. Her ma had the right idea of covering her mouth with a floury hand.

"Keep your voice *down!*" Ma whispered in a sharp hiss. She kneeled beside Ailís, bewildered beyond words. Her gaze flashed between her daughter's eyes and the hatchling still slithering out its shell, trailing some type of viscous goop in its wake. And she had just cleaned the floors earlier that morning.

Ailís continued to croon her excitement despite being muffled by her mother's hand. She was probably saying something to the effect of, "But, Ma! It's a real, actual dragon!" but it instead came across as, "*Bmmh, Mm! Ihs a rhl, ashml drngnhn!*"

"I will *not* have the Inquisition knocking down our door just because you brought home a...where did you even find this egg, to begin with?" She removed her hand from Ailís's mouth, caution evident on her face.

Rather than answer the question, Ailís watched the final length of the silver dragon emerge from the egg, its tail meeting the floor with enough of a thud to startle, its scales scraping the ground with enough shrill force to irritate. Ailís didn't care, though. Her heart was aflutter. There was not a chance that this little thing could be capable of great evil as the Inquisition would have told her. It was just...a little guy. A fact only emphasized as it opened its eyes and met Ailís's gaze.

A tinny noise escaped the dragon's mouth, something resembling a bird's squawk but with none of the melody.

Ailís felt her smile widen to the point of straining her cheeks. She reached her hands out to the creature, enticing it to approach. For the briefest of moments, it appeared that the dragon was to take her up on the offer, only for her to be pulled up to her feet by her wrists and turned around, her ma clasping at her shoulders.

"We can*not* have a..." Ma looked to her left and right, seeming to listen for any armored footsteps outside the door. She lowered her voice as she leaned in closer to Ailís. "...a *dragon* in this house, or anywhere near us! Do you understand what it could do to us?"

"But, Ma, just look at him!" Ailís pleaded. "He couldn't hurt a fly!"

"Oh, it's a 'he,' now, is it?"

Ailís shrugged. "I'unno. How do you check?"

Ma blinked in a moment of silence, and then appeared averse to addressing that question at all (and perhaps would revisit it in a few years). "It can't hurt a thing because it's *two minutes old*."

The quiet smile remained on Ailís's face. She had nothing to add to that; all she wanted was to watch the dragon slither about the floor. And that's what she did, leaving her mother sputtering with frustration.

Camaráin also made his way over and laid in front of the hatchling, resting his chin atop his folded hands. He said nothing, but, judging from the glint of excitement in his eyes, he was no less enthralled by the creature's presence. A soft smile stretched across his lips as he watched the dragon's movements.

"It can't stay here." Ma brought herself down to the children's level, her brow furrowed, strands of hair trailing in front of her eyes. The gesture usually meant she was three degrees of separation from pulling out all her hair. The children loved bringing her to that point, willingly or no.

Ailís began to protest with wide eyes. "But, M—"

"But *nothing*! The Inquisition is always listening, they are always watching, and they always appear when you least expect it."

"I think we could expect it," Camaráin muttered with a shrug. "They're loud enough to expect."

"No one expects the Inquisition of the Priory of the Thrice-Dead Prophet!"

"No one has the time."

"Regardless," Ma snapped. "I don't need to stress what they'll do not only to that dragon if they find it, but what they'll do to *us*!"

"But why would they do anything to him, Ma?" Ailís asked. She held out a hand to the hatchling. "Look at him!"

"Need I ask you where your uncle Iósaf is now?" Ma's eyes were stern.

Meanwhile, Ailís was confused. "Why would you ask me? Why would I know?"

Ma buried her face in her hands, a rasped and frustrated

groan screamed into her palms.

Taking her mother's disinclination toward words at the moment, Ailís decided to lay on the ground, bringing herself eye-level with the dragon. She was entranced by his icy grey eyes and he seemed similarly enthralled with hers. He tilted his head as he stared at Ailís as though he were a curious dog, and extended for the first time its small wings, breaking off the scales of his back.

"Even if we *could* do something about him..." Ailís began, not looking up at her ma. (Likely a good call.) "There are probably too many Inquisitors walking around right now, so...can we keep him? Please? Please, please, please?"

"Oh, Heaven help me," Ma muttered under her breath.

Ailís jumped with excitement, nearly tripping over the hem of her skirt. "That's not a no!" She turned and skipped over to the bottom cabinets, rifling through them, and chucking unwanted items off to the side without regard for her surroundings.

"What are you doing, Ailís?" Ma asked. She sounded defeated. She was tired of being defeated by a precocious eleven-year-old.

Humming to herself, Ailís withdrew a wicker picnic basket from the rear of the cabinet. "I'm gonna pick some flowers and berries and we're gonna bake a pie because we're gonna throw him a birthday party!" Before she could hear any objections, Ailís sprinted for the door, her ma's frustrated shout only briefly audible before the girl slammed the door shut. Faintly, she could still hear the muffled ravings that Camaráin was now forced to endure.

As was often the job of the younger sibling.

A meadow extended not too far from the house. It was one of Ailís's favorite spots to hide when the time came to avoid responsibilities. Purple swaths of heather stretched to the west, while plots of red clovers and cowslips were planted years back as a means for folk to pick and gift them without needing to travel in search of them.

Beyond the rows of heather lay a bramble where wild blackberries would grow, and luckily it was the time of year they were plenty ripe. Ailís could scarcely count all the times she'd come home with fingers stained purple from indulging in too many berries. Those were simpler times, a week ago.

With a grin, she sifted through the various plots and picked the flowers that looked the most vibrant to her, and then skipped along to the bramble of blackberries. One would go into the basket, one into her mouth, one in the basket, three in her mouth, and so on. After enough time had passed, she neglected to fill her still-empty basket, but one can hardly help themselves when given the opportunity to devour fresh Nóran blackberries. There had been a shortage in recent years in Baile, and Ailís was likely the cause.

With the bramble thoroughly scoured for the best berries—and her stomach thoroughly filled with those same best berries— Ailís looked down to see that she had enough berries for...something that could be considered a pie.

"Good enough!" she exclaimed and turned back to the village. Sprigs of heather danced out of her basket with each excited step, but it was not within her to mind. There was cause to celebrate and celebrate she would!

"What has you so giddy, wee one?" a voice asked as she skipped by.

Ailís half-turned and began to speak, the smile still wide on her face. "We're gonna bake a pie because we—"

Few sights could keep Ailís quiet, but the presence of an Inquisitor was always one of them. A man clad in heavy armor, minus a helmet, approached her as she froze in place, his metallic steps sinking into the soft ground underneath him. His face was beset by wrinkles that traveled all the way up his forehead, which drew attention to his receding hairline. He offered her a smile, but it looked unnatural from how wide his mouth stretched.

"...really like pie?" Ailís finished.

The Inquisitor towered over her. Why the Inquisition insisted its flock remain in full armor even in these midland farming villages was beyond Ailís's understanding, but this particular one looked out of place. The disparity of his mismatched teeth and lazy eyes (yes, both of them) against his glittering armor was pronounced. Emblazoned on his breastplate was the sigil of the Priory of the Thrice-Dead Prophet—a fellow who had clearly died three times—with the emblem of the Inquisition—a cracked dragon egg—hastily added atop it. The formality of the man's armor contrasted with the smears of mud on his face.

And yet, Ailís was intimidated by his presence just the same. She managed a nervous smile, but she could still feel herself shaking.

Crossing his arms—awkwardly, it should be noted, as his vambraces and gauntlets were far too big for him—the Inquisitor looked at her with a hint of undeserved self-importance. He seemed to be considering Ailís's words for far too long.

"I hope you plan on helping your ma with baking that pie,"

he said, his voice far too nasally to match the intimidation he was trying to instill.

Ailís felt it just the same. She nodded. "Yes, sir."

"And you'll help her clean as well, I trust?"

"Yes, sir." Rarely did she help clean, but there was no use in lying.

The Inquisitor nodded. "Enjoy your pie, then." He walked away, back to resuming whatever patrol he was on.

It took the spring out of Ailís's step, to be sure. She always did her best to avoid the Inquisition where she could. Her uncle had often told her of the misplaced importance each Inquisitor always had in themselves, especially where the laws of the land were concerned. Every village and town throughout Nóra were forced to have Inquisitors stationed within, despite the fact that, one, they did not carry out the law of the land; two, their supposed "mission" had been accomplished all those generations ago (though, with the hatching of a new dragon, it was clear they didn't do a good job); and, three, the Priory had no actual military arm, and the Inquisition was co-opting the sigil of another and attaching themselves to the religious sect for the name recognition.

Not that that meant much to Ailís when she was five years old, but if there was one thing she remembered about her uncle, it was that he would rant to anyone who would listen. She wondered who he was ranting to now, and where.

But she had wasted enough time cowering. It was time to bake a pie.

Which meant that it was time for her ma to bake a pie.

"I'm not baking a pie," Ma said once Ailís returned.

Ailís frowned, dropping the basket to the floor. Loose

heather and violets fell off the rim, and there was a slight splat as the bottom layer of blackberries burst. With the mess impending, Ailís looked at the hatchling, who was still crawling about the floor. "But Ma!"

"But, *nothing*, Ailís." Exasperation colored Ma's tone. She looked exhausted past the point of anger.

"We have to do *something* for him, though!" The volume in Ailís's voice wavered, forgetting and remembering the need for discretion.

"What we *have* to do is get rid of it."

"I'll keep him a secret."

"That is *not* the issue."

Ailís scampered over to the dragon and picked him up, the hatchling slithering initially as though with fright, but quickly settling into her palms. He was heavier than she had expected. "But look at him!"

Ma did not, but Camaráin did. He was sitting cross-legged in the corner, reading a book that Uncle Iósaf had left here years ago entitled, *Gnomes, Faeries, Selkies, and Other Fae Creatures Approved by High Inquisitor Dónal That Aren't Evil Dragons.* The lettering was too large for the cover and whoever penned the book had begun to make the words smaller and smaller so it would all fit. She had to squint to see the word "Dragons."

"Can't we just bake him a pie, Ma?" Ailís continued. "Please?"

"I already told you. I'm not baking a pie for that thing, and I want it out of the house *now*."

With a huff, Ailís walked over to her brother and placed the dragon beside him for safe-keeping before going back to her basket. "Then I'll bake a pie!"

Ma shook her head with annoyance. "Ailís, you don't know how."

Ailís wanted to match her mother's annoyance—as young children are wont to do when they believe they know better than their mothers—but the negativity melted away when she glanced upon the dragon, who had nuzzled Camaráin's leg. "Well, I don't think there's a better time to learn than now," she said with confidence.

The confidence lasted about twenty seconds.

Chapter Three

As it turned out, baking was more difficult than Ma had made it out to be.

While getting the fire going in the oven was easy enough—and Ma had been alarmed at how easily she could start a fire—Ailís was stumped at what to do next. She'd watched her mother bake a hundred pies and she'd eaten a hundred and one.

The realization hit her that it was never the art of baking that enthralled her; it was simply the anticipation there would soon be baked goods that had kept her captivated.

With no other options, Ailís coated the baking tin in a layer of blackberries, covered them in flour, and then threw them in the oven and hoped for the best.

Ignoring her mother's shaking head and paying no heed to the smell of burning berries, Ailís returned to her wicker basket, withdrew some sprigs of heather and tied them together with red clovers and cowslips like jewels in a crown. She looked at the dragon, who still rested his newborn head against Camaráin's leg, and tiptoed over, careful not to rouse the hatchling from his slumber.

She held the flower crown up to the dragon's head and

huffed, overestimating how large his skull would be, leaving herself with a flower arrangement three times the size it need-ed to be. With a shrug, she placed the crown atop her brother's head, though it was a size or two too small. Camaráin paid little heed, and Ailís wondered if he even recognized that she placed something atop his head to begin with.

The stench of burned berries grew worse and smoke was billowing out of the oven. Meanwhile, Ailís made a smaller flower crown. It was the perfect size for the newborn dragon. Everything was going perfectly.

Eventually—and before the house burned down—Ma pulled the smoking tin out of the oven. Rolling her eyes, she announced, "Ailís, your..." She gestured, her daughter's cre-ation not resembling what one would call a pie. "...is ready."

With great caution to not wake him, Ailís placed the crown atop the dragon's head and skipped over to the baking tin, thanking her mother for retrieving it while she tended to her other tasks. The anticipation of baked goods gripped her as she looked in the tin.

Her anticipation remained as she wondered if her pie was hiding under the mixture of crisped and liquified berries and loose flour. Deep down, Ailís supposed there *had* to have been further steps to the baking process, but she was nonetheless disappointed at seeing no flaky crust and smelling no enchant-ing aroma, unless the stench of burned fruit counted toward the latter. Her previous attempt at baking, some weeks prior, had instead produced something as black as tar and smelling just as foul, so this was hardly the worst of her creations, and she took solace in that it at least looked like the filling she was going for...kind of. Far be it for her to give the hatchling any false notions that his first meal was a disappointment.

Despite Ma's angry, twitching lip—something about ruining the bottom of the tin that she half-tuned out—Ailís took her creation and carried it over to the dragon. The smell (not quite an aroma, not nearly a stench) woke him and he started sniffing the contents with curiosity, the flower crown remaining balanced on his head as he did so. A long, thin tongue slithered out of his mouth and began licking her attempted pie. At first, Ailís was concerned about the pieless filling being too hot, but the hatchling hardly seemed to mind. In fact, from the enthusiasm with which he took bite after bite, he seemed quite enamored with the creation, heat and all.

Triumph filling her, Ailís turned to her ma and said, "See? He likes it!" She put her hands on her hips, a wide smile stretching her lips. "I guess I'm pretty good at this baking thing!"

Tremors gripped Ma's hands, her face turning a deeper red. Ailís couldn't tell if she was angry or simply unwell.

Rather than revealing which, Ma turned on her heel and left the house.

Shrugging, Ailís thought nothing further of it and returned her focus to the dragon, who still seemed to be enjoying the primordial soup she had managed to create.

Camaráin looked up from his book and opened his mouth to speak before being distracted by the flower crown on his head. Evidently, he *hadn't* noticed earlier. He took it off, glanced at it, and tossed it aside, and then said, "We should give him a name."

"A name?" Ailís craned her head. "We can do that?"

"There are a lot of names in this book," Camaráin said, holding up the Inquisition's heavy anti-draconic tome with shaking hands. "This chapter is just called, 'EVIL' in bold print and the only thing in it is names of dragons the High Inquisitor decided to list, but there's Bykilth, Eoldroig, Zassein, Paarthurnax, Smaug, Miezus, Toothless…"

With a quick giggle, Ailís instead proposed, "We should call him Pilib." Even when met with silence, Ailís found herself thoroughly amused. She picked the dragon up and held it at eye level. "What do you think, little guy? Do you like the name Pilib?"

The dragon—Pilib—opened his mouth wide in what appeared to be a smile but could very well have been a desire to eat more of the mystery slop. Ailís indulged him either way.

While Camaráin continued to disregard the simple, human name given to the dragon in deference to reciting further names from the so-called chapter of evil, Ailís was more than content to place the hatchling back in front of the tin and watch him devour his hatch-day treat. It was impressive, the sight of him so joyfully devouring what most would describe as "inedible," a "disaster," or "ruining my baking tin."

So if there was one thing Pilib the dragon taught Ailís, it was that dragons enjoyed mystery slop, which was probably one thing she knew that the High Inquisitor did not.

Chapter Four

The encroaching night was disheartening, to say the least.

It was impossible to predict that his travels through the village of Baile would be such an ordeal, but Liam had the aches, stench, and disgruntled horses to prove it. He could still feel what he hoped was mud in his hair, a fire roared up leg from where he landed in the street, his head pulsed with red-hot fury, and his pride had taken a wounding from the stern talking-to that Inquisitor had given him, even though he, thankfully, did not decide to inspect his wagon. Also, one of the horses bit his finger.

And that didn't account for the work that needed to be done on the wagon's wheels before he could take it anywhere. The rear axle had a crack in it and the right rear wheel was misaligned to the point of uselessness. It was to Liam's good fortune there were several carpenters willing to help him on such short notice. One of the benefits of these backwater midland villages.

If only he thought to ask about that girl he saw poorly hiding from him in the village market before he found himself swimming in mud. An issue for later.

He was ready for the day to be over. The lavish estate looming on the horizon was all the relief he needed to put this horrid day behind him.

Why anyone of wealth would settle in these boglands was beyond Liam's ken, but he had enough of an inkling from his correspondence with Lord Saibhir to gather that he was a man of eccentric tastes. Somehow, the land around the estate looked pristine and untouched, the area within its gated confines lined with mesmerizing fields of green that glittered in the waning light. At the end of the pathway was a mansion—no, a *palace* would be the correct word. Liam had seen much of the land of Nóra in his travels, from the harsh beauty of the Cliffs of Ard to the manic bustle of the southern ports, but that anyone had the means to construct a dwelling of such magnanimity on this isle was unheard of. It was three stories of carved stone, the length of the village of Baile, and if Liam were a betting man, one could shove every Nóran into this estate and it still would be nowhere near full.

And, there were only two guards at the gate, and no one patrolling within. Aesthetics mattered more than manpower.

"Ho, there!" the guard on the left shouted as Liam approached in his carriage. At his hip lay the hilt of a sword. There was no sword attached to it, but he still rested his hand atop the pommel all the same.

Tired though he was, Liam still managed a hearty smile as the guards drew near. "Evening, lads. Name's Liam, believe the lord has been expecting me."

The second sentry lifted the bill of his dingy and dented helmet and eyed the merchant was suspicion. "You was expected hours ago. Lord Saibhir's been right mad 'bout it." He crossed his arms, probably to exhibit some measure of toughness, but from the awkward angle of the motion, it was not lost upon Liam that he was trying to hide a large tear in his leather cuirass. A quick look at his hip showed a scabbard with a blade, but no hilt. Together, these two could have made a functioning knight. It was all the confirmation Liam needed that this Saibhir was far more wont to spend his wealth on his person than on his protection.

"My deepest apologies to your lord," Liam responded with a bow, almost deep enough for him to tip over. Again. The horses appeared ready to rear their legs in "fright" should he have done so. "Ran into some trouble over in Baile. Some folks there saw me straight and sent me on my way. Else I'd've been here hours ago."

"Good folk over in Baile. Used to live there afore Lord Saibhir took us in, we did," the bladeless guard said. A wide smile revealed he was also half-toothless.

Liam nodded, impressed at someone from Baile being brought on to guard an estate of this grandeur in the first place. Though if what they had on their person was their own prior to coming into Lord Saibhir's service, that could very well have explained much about the danger, or lack thereof, these lands presented. He looked at the other guard, whose smile revealed a full row of teeth. They truly did complete one another.

"Well, lads," he said. "I'm loath to anger Lord Saibhir any further than I already have. If I could just make my way in to see him..."

"'Course, 'course!" the hiltless guard exclaimed. "Pardon our delayin' ya. I'll run right in and grab him." And true to his word, he opened the gates and sprinted toward the mansion doors, some half-mile away. No want for enthusiasm on that one.

The other guard gestured Liam inside, and the merchant nudged his horses forward to follow. Ol' Bladeless whistled a tuneless melody with his hands in his pockets as Liam trailed in tow, appearing unperturbed by the fact he left the gate open with no one to guard it. It was the middle of nowhere, true, but to Liam, it felt like poor decorum.

The slow stroll gave Liam plenty of time to take in the decorations adorning the lawn, everything from beautifully carved marble statues to what looked to be animal skeletons restored to their original form. Many of which were species Liam was fairly certain were extinct. Recently extinct, even. One within the last half-year. It was strange not seeing that flightless bird around anymore. One could only wonder...

A loud groan caught his attention. The front doors creaked open, themselves bearing the resemblance of massive shields guarding against those who'd wish to enter. The shields probably could have been made for the two guards for a lot less money, but Liam was hardly one to argue with the whims of the wealthy so long as they paid him.

The illusion of grandeur was broken, if only for a moment, by the return of the other sentry, red in the face and slick with sweat. How far he had to run was a mystery to Liam. For all he knew, the rear of the mansion could have stretched all the way to the sea.

Through ragged breaths, the guard shouted, or rather, wheezed out, "Pre...presentin'...His Lord...ship...Lord Saibhir!" He fell face-first on the graveled pathway, the one stretch of land in the estate not composed of grass.

If the assumption of wealth had vanished with the reappearance of the guard, it had returned when Lord Saibhir emerged. The folk in the village of Baile were a bit on the skinnier side in Liam's view, and Saibhir was probably the cause of it by the look of him. Grand in both air and girth, the lord approached Liam with an expression of self-importance. He carried a thick build, especially around the waistline, despite how much he attempted to conceal it with fine silks, furs, wool, cottons, and other clashing fabrics. Liam had never visited the mainland to the southeast, but all he had read of the nobility on the continent was that they exuded excess and embellishment. Saibhir looked plucked from that flock, out of place entirely in the more modest confines of Nóra.

Liam was at a loss for how to carry himself, so he settled for a deep bow. "Lord Saibhir, a pleasure to at last make your acquaintance." When he looked up, he found himself peering into the man's nostrils for how high Saibhir had turned his nose.

"Your tardiness has disrupted my schedule," he announced in a booming voice, his jowls jiggling. "My bi-hourly meal and bath was nearly run aground."

"And you have my deepest apologies, my lord," Liam answered. "I ran into some unexpected complications in Baile, but I—"

"You have run my schedule afoul," Saibhir interrupted.

Liam stopped with mouth agape. With deliberate enunciation, he said, "Then I must voice how sorry I am. As I traipsed through the village of Baile, unforeseen circumstances prevented my intended arrival." If Saibhir could say the same thing twice, then so could he.

"Hmm. Just so." An in-drawn breath rasped in the back of his throat.

Liam threw his hands out at his side, befuddled. Flowery, nonsense words were apparently more comprehensible to the man.

"Had you arrived but half an hour later," Saibhir continued, "our business arrangement would have been no more. Consider yourself fortunate that I still deign to allow it. I conduct my dealings in a certain manner, and from my partners, I expect the same."

The sight of the collapsed guard in the gravel would have suggested the contrary, but Liam managed to hold his tongue. "Then I would ask for a second chance at a first impression, my lord. Allow it, and your already magnanimous fortune will grow all the more."

Saibhir crossed his arms. "You have the manner of speech of a man far above your station."

"Thank you, my lord."

"It was not a compliment."

"Oh, sod it." Liam had suffered far too many pains today to endure this inane war of words. "I've brought what you requested. Might we get on with this?"

The lord plodded over toward the wagon. "I would inspect the cargo personally before our business continues." He did not look at Liam as he passed by.

"Very good, sir, be my guest," Liam said. Even with his aches, he still sped past the waddling lord to open the rear of the wagon. After waiting a few long moments for Saibhir to join him, he gestured to the interior. "Everything you requested, sir. Freshly skinned pelts, excavated skeletons, a northern chef, a combination of all three, those were all easy to get. But I do hope you appreciate the effort to procure...these." He reached for the large, ornate box embossed with gold knots, his merchant's smile wide. Presentation was everything for these unusual requests he had undertaken over the years. Some would disregard the goods if they arrived in something so simple as a burlap sack, regardless of the item's value. He knew from experience, and he still avoided the southeast whenever he could because of it. It was no small feat to procure this box for presentation purposes, though whether his liaising with the governor's daughter—and the resulting threats on his life—was worth the effort of obtaining it remained to be seen.

But the moment he pulled the box forward, he noticed something was amiss. In his haste to depart Baile after the repairs to his wagon were completed, he neglected to inspect everything in full. Had he done so, he would have noticed the snapped lock on the box...and he also would have noticed that it was empty.

"Well?" Where Saibhir's voice had done little more than annoy Liam previously, it now instilled a terror he had not before experienced in all his years of ~~smuggling~~ legitimate trade and commerce. "Do you have the eggs, or do you not?"

With pronounced hesitation, Liam pushed the empty box back into the wagon as though it hadn't existed at all. He met Lord Saibhir's eyes, and he did not need daylight to discern the radiant glow of anger on his face. Slowly, Liam folded his hands in front of him, a sinking feeling settling in his gut. He drew a deep breath, had a long think about what next to say, and came up with:

"Can I interest you in any of my insurance plans in the case of lost or stolen items?"

Chapter Five

The stories Uncle Iósaf recited to Ailís growing up stuck with her for years. Sometimes she had dreams about riding atop a dragon, soaring through the skies above Nóra and beyond, a world of wonders ready to unfold before her, the glittering horizons not a mystery but a destination.

Last night's dreams carried her to those same faraway shores, but not atop a dragon. For once, Ailís *was* the dragon, her wings spread wide as she rode the wind. The air was so dense she could grasp it and direct its movements. She was at one with and in complete control of nature itself.

Even when she awoke, an echo of the sensation remained tingling in her hands like pins and needles as though she fallen asleep against both arms and they were slowing waking back up. Needless to say, it was the strangest dream she ever had.

She may have been concerned had it not been for Pilib nuzzling her in her bed, the hatchling still asleep and even snoring. His crown of flowers had remained atop his head throughout the night, filling Ailís's nose with a pleasant perfume. It put her heart at ease, and the strange feeling from her dream subsided. Smiling, she gently caressed the rough scales of Pilib's neck. She wondered if this was the same way a mother felt when holding her newborn.

"You're finally up," a voice called from the doorway, breaking Ailís from her reverie.

If the feeling Ailís felt toward Pilib was that of a mother and her baby, the expression on Ma's face was indicative of a mother who probably had that feeling long ago...but hadn't gotten a restful night's sleep in the eleven years since. Dark bags drooped beneath her eyes, cracks stretching across her eyes from her pupils like red lightning, her face a shade paler than normal. Usually when this happened, Ma had a bad headache and an upset stomach, but she wasn't sick, and wouldn't elaborate any further. Usually, the explanation was followed by, "You'll understand when you have kids."

Ailís wondered if she'd understand with Pilib.

"It's still here then, is it?" she asked, inclining her head toward the dragon.

On reflex, Ailís ran her hand down Pilib's head. The hatchling began to rouse from his slumber. Ailís nodded, holding the dragon close to her chest, already reluctant to let him go. "Uh-huh," she said. "Please, Ma? He hasn't caused any trouble. He even cleaned the bottom of the baking tin!"

The baking tin, in fact, looked much worse.

Ma closed her eyes for so long, Ailís thought she may have fallen asleep on her feet. Then came a furious sigh. She took a deliberate step inside Ailís's room.

Ailís gripped Pilib even tighter, the dragon squawking and grumbling in response. "Think about how much Uncle Iósaf would have loved him if he was here. He's behaving and he's not bothering anyone. Why can't we keep him?" Tears welled in her eyes. An attempt at manipulation? No, she would *never*.

Regardless, it didn't work. The mention of Iósaf only seemed to deepen Ma's frustration. As she reached Ailís's bed, she knelt on the floor, folding her hands before her. "It does not matter if it did nothing to disrupt our house in one day," she said with slow enunciation, the voice she adopted when she needed to remind the children of the authority they repeatedly ignored. "All it takes is one thing—*one* thing—to happen for the Inquisition to be kicking down our doors and ruining our lives forever. Whatever my brother would feel toward this *thing*—" She gestured toward Pilib with a tinge of malice coating her words. "—is irrelevant. He's gone because he thought he knew more than the Inquisition. If he'd kept his curiosity in check, he'd still be with us today." Ma stopped, a frown creasing her lips. Her anger broke enough to reveal a pang of worry and sadness shrouded beneath the mask. "Frankly, that wild rebelliousness of his is something the two of you share too much of."

With a quivering lip and a chill running up her arms, Ailís opened her mouth to speak.

"No," Ma interrupted, holding up a finger before Ailís could get a word in. "Now, I don't know where you found this egg, or how it ended up in our village to begin with, or why it exists in the first place. But the Inquisitors are dumb beasts with a singular goal and no compunctions about being polite or asking questions. It may not be today, it may not be tomorrow, but sooner or later, the Inquisition is going to catch wind of this thing in our house, and then there will be a knock at our door."

There was a knock at the door.

"Goddamn it."

The reality of the situation set in for the first time, and Ailís's tears, once a tool for master manipulation, became those of fear and regret. Her lip quivered, but again, Ma put a finger to them before she could say a word.

Ma brought her voice low, as near to yelling at her daughter as she could while still keeping it to a sharp whisper. "This conversation is not over. Hide it, make sure it doesn't slither on out. Stay where you are. Do you understand me?"

Ailís nodded. Being so agreeable was not something to which she was accustomed, but she hid Pilib amongst her stuffed dolls all the same. He blended in well enough with the bears and wolves and other animals who were actually known to be a danger to people.

Though she opted to heed the warning to remain hidden, she couldn't deny her curiosity and peeked her head around the threshold as her ma answered the door, which had initially been a steady staccato rhythm but quickly shifted to a discordant pounding.

Ma opened the door and the Inquisitor nearly fell across the threshold. He was different from the Inquisitor who had questioned Ailís the day before. For one, he actually looked the part. Secondly, he was so tall that his head was almost out of view. And third, the mean expression on the visible half of his face was natural, an impression Ailís did not have of most of the village's Inquisitors, who often looked the type to practice their angry faces in the mirror every morning. This man could very well have been the sole competent member in the whole of the Inquisition.

"Good morning, Máirín," he said in greeting, his voice a deep grumble.

"Yes, yes, good morning to you as well, Eamon," Ma replied,

very much ill-inclined to match the Inquisitor's courtesy. Ailís didn't know any of the Inquisitors by name, but he must have been enough of a regular in the village for Ma to know his and he to know hers. "What do you need?"

Eamon held up his hands in a placating gesture, an image of subversion that ran counter to his menacing appearance. "Is this a bad time? I can return later if you would prefer."

"I have two young children, Eamon. There's never a good time."

Silence, and then he nodded. Or so Ailís assumed. Again, it was impossible for her to see his head. "Rough night?"

"I have two young children, Eamon," she repeated, as though that was the answer to everything. To be fair, in most instances, it was. "Now, what is it? I need to get the kids ready."

Ailís craned an eyebrow, unaware of what there was to get ready for.

"Right, then," Eamon muttered, the gravel in his voice overtaking the prior courtesy. "Word has spread of draconic contraband finding its way to Baile. You know full well that means we're duty-bound to ask questions accordingly, so the policy remains the same as ever: if you see something..."

"Yes, yes, say something," Ma finished. If there was any hint of knowing in her face, she was hiding it well. Ailís always liked that about her. Ma was good at keeping secrets (except for when it had to do with gifts, which had remained in the same hiding place in the cupboard for about eight years). "What is it this time? Scales, wings, candlewax marketed as 'liquid dragonfire' again?"

"If only it were so easy this time." Eamon chuckled. "No, believe it or not, there have supposedly been...eggs in our midst."

Ma scoffed. "Eggs? The dragons are gone, aren't they?"

(The Inquisition paradox again rearing its ugly head.)

"Well...nothing is ever really *gone*, is it?"

A noncommittal grunt provided enough of an answer. Ma's body language was as stern as ever. She was not breaking. Ailís liked that. "So, who's the offender now? What's brought the Inquisition to another uproar?"

"Lord Saibhir, actually."

"Huh." Ma seemed taken aback by that. "Shouldn't you all be...arresting him, then, or whatever it is you do?"

Ailís had heard the name Saibhir before but had never seen him. All she knew was that he was the governor of the Nóran midlands, though what he actually *did* was beyond her reckoning.

Eamon shrugged. "Well...he doesn't actually *have* the eggs, so our jurisdiction over his dealings ends there."

"Then why is he causing such an uproar?"

"Our sources tell us he was...supposed to have them. A black market dealer was also rumored to have been here yesterday harboring the said contraband. But, well..."

"Neither party has them." Ma finished. There was an edge to her words. One that Ailís knew meant she should go back to hiding in earnest. She did just that, sidling against the bedroom wall but still keeping a curious ear on the conversation.

"Correct," Eamon confirmed.

"And you cannot question either Lord Saibhir or this black market dealer because these eggs are not in their possession."

"Got it in one."

"And you, as an Inquisitor, can do nothing if so-called 'draconic contraband' is not present, yes?"

"Mm-hmm."

"And you have no legal power otherwise?"

"R...right."

"Then what purpose do you serve by being here?"

Ailís's eyes widened at the bluntness of the question. For all her ma's posturing of the dangers of the Inquisition...she sure was pointing out how *un*dangerous they were.

"Um...well...not much, I suppose."

"Thought as much."

"Right, well. Have a good day, Máir—"

The door slammed shut. Footsteps followed. If there was one lesson Ailís had learned from her ma, it was that there was no escape during these moments. She knew she was in trouble. Drawing a deep breath, she braced herself for her Ma's impending screams. Her eyes remained frozen on her stuffed animals—and Pilib—who all seemed to laugh at her imminent misery.

When the footsteps ended, Ailís knew she had to look to her left. The anger on Ma's face told the story.

"So," Ma began, her voice cold as ice. "What's this about *multiple* eggs that have gone missing?"

Furrowing her brow, Ailís crossed her arms and said, "I don't know! I only took the one—oops." She quickly covered her mouth.

Ma grunted. "Well," she began, her voice cold as ice. "I'm sure you still have a story to tell me of how you came home with *one* dragon egg?"

Ailís *could* have regaled her with the gripping tale of how she played a prank on a peddler—who as it turned out was likely a black market merchant anyway—broke his wagon, upset his horses, watched him hurt himself as he landed in the mud, all the while a stray dragon egg fell out of his cargo and wound up in her grasp. *But*, if he was harboring an egg illegally (or possibly multiple eggs), was she not performing a service by preventing a foul economic service to prevail?

So, instead, she elected to smile at her ma and not say a word. Silence was certainly the best option. It wasn't lying if she said nothing. It wasn't telling the truth, either, but there was no need to get into the semantics of it all.

Ma knew the game. She'd been playing it for far too long, and the score had long been weighted in Ailís's favor. She folded an arm across her body and buried her face in the opposite palm. One more point for the youngster.

"*That*," she said, pointing at Pilib, whose scaled face did not blend in at all among the stuffed animals, "still needs to go." Ma paused for a second, but then loosed another defeated sigh. "But you're late for dance practice again, and you're not missing another one."

Ailís pouted.

"Don't give me that. The big recital's tomorrow, and I'm not going to be held accountable for your delinquency again. Get changed, throw your shoes on, then we're *going*."

And that was that. Finally, a point for Ma. Ailís rose to her feet without further protest and rummaged through the clothing pile in the corner of the room. Pilib maintained a watchful and curious eye as she changed clothes, and all Ailís could think as she did so was soaring through the sky, the wind at her command, and all the liberty there for the taking.

Barring any miracles, she doubted that would happen today.

Chapter Six

The rhythm of the bodhran thumped while the fiddler filled the air with their enchanting melody, but Ailís could find the enjoyment in none of it. Hiding amongst the throng of the more attuned members of her dancing cohort, she hoped the lack of rigidity to her posture and the out-of-step sequencing to her slip-jig would go unnoticed by the instructor. Miss Róisín was already cross with her arrival (and Ailís had to wonder if the instructor would be lessso had she elected not to show at all), so there was a risk of wrath should the young dance not have moved with the light, airy grace expected of her.

Ailís struggled to keep her heart in it. No, scratch that. She never had the heart for it, and longed for the day when Ma would allow her the option to continue on with the step dancing or not. A lifetime of clicking ankles suffered from years of tapping her feet in nine-eighths time didn't sound nice. Even less so under the hawkish eye of Miss Róisín.

It was the distractions of home that kept Ailís otherwise occupied. She wondered how much longer she could keep Pilib before Ma forced her to rid themselves of the dragon. Worry filled her that she would return from her lessons to find the hatchling already gone without being allowed the opportunity to bid him farewell. She knew Ma was adamant about it, especially with the cloud of the Inquisition threatening them from above.

Feelings of anger toward the Inquisition manifested in earnest. Uncle Iósaf's lectures about them had always lingered in Ailís's mind—everything from the pointlessness of their being in modern Nóran society to their general gullibility. Those were *frequent* topics to the extent that Ailís could recite the words verbatim for how much they were repeated—as well as Ma's rebukes for him to stop pestering the dairy farmer and to "just buy the milk, you numpty."

But for the first time since Uncle Iósaf's disappearance, Ailís felt she had legitimate cause for her anger toward the Inquisition. Here was the first dragon seen south of the Highlands in generations, content with eating a freshly baked(?) blackberry pie(?) and cozying up beside her in bed, and the Inquisitors would consider him *evil*? It wasn't right.

Even as her feet managed to keep in some approximation of the correct sequencing with her fellow dancers, the desire to play with Pilib as much as she could before the inevitable came to pass was all she could think about. He still needed a proper birthday party, as well. Once Ma warmed up to him, anyway. *If* she did.

So lost in thought was Ailís that she didn't realize the music had stopped about two minutes ago, but her feet did not get the memo. A circle had formed around her by the time she noticed, several of the girls already with cups of water. Someone in the background clapped out a rhythm resembling that of Ailís's feet, though she had long since abandoned the correct time-keeping for the slip-jig and devolved (or *evolved*, depending on one's perspective) into an intricate and progressive alternation between the timestamps of four-fourths, seven-eighths, three-fourths, and thirteen-sixteenths.

Miss Róisín displayed a disapproving frown when Ailís finally stopped. "Is there a song in your heart you'd rather we play, Ailís?" Strands of curled, red hair drifted in line with her dark, green eyes, encasing them in enough shadow to resemble a portal to Hell below. Most folk in Baile didn't fear the Inquisition; they feared Miss Róisín instead.

Sweat trickled down Ailís's face as she struggled to catch her breath—and struggled to look her instructor in the eyes. "No...ma'am. Sorry, Miss...Miss Róisín. I was a little...distracted."

"See that you aren't tomorrow while the whole village watches."

Ailís gulped. "No, ma'am. I won't be."

The instructor grunted. Miss Róisín turned and snapped her fingers at the musicians in the corner. "Line up! You lot, from the top!" As Ailís reassumed her position in the middle of the group, Miss Róisín, without turning around, shouted, "No, Ailís, up front with you! Best you get in your practice for staying on task with all the eyes of the village upon you."

Hanging her head low, Ailís muttered, "Yes, ma'am." She pushed past the rows, her ghillies clacking against the floor. As the fiddler indicated their need for an extra minute in order to tune their strings, Ailís looked at the ground rather than at of her instructor, wishing and hoping for this lesson to be over as soon as possible. However many minutes she had remaining with Pilib were ones she wanted to treasure.

The wish came half-true, at least. The music began again, the bodhran thumped, and the light grace of the slip-jig demanded Ailís's attention, but she lost her focus when she saw Camaráin sidling in through the doorway, his mop of light brown hair swaying as he bobbed his head to the lively melody. Slung over his shoulder was his wool messenger bag, and a bulge shuffled along its confines as though trying to break out, desperate for an exit.

The desperation paid off as Pilib's scaly face popped out from under the flap for a brief moment, his mouth opened wide in an approximation of a smile.

Ailís's answering smile was wide, and she skipped over to the new arrivals, even as Camaráin shoved Pilib's face back into his bag before anyone noticed his presence.

Silence fell over the hall as the music stopped, all movement ceased, several hissed breaths drawn inward.

"Ailís," Miss Róisín called, ice in her tone. "What did I say about not getting distracted?"

Despite the looming threat of the dance instructor, Ailís continued to approach her brother, humming a tune to match the dance she had just created. "Sorry, ma'am! Just shooing my brother. You've said the performance should be a surprise for the village, right?" The exact wording involved language her Ma had forbidden her from ever repeating, though the prior proclamation had caused two of the girls to cry and another to foul herself. They were never seen again.

Miss Róisín didn't offer a response but judging from the reduced tension permeating through the room, it seemed she was deterred well enough.

Camaráin's brow furrowed in a manner showing concern as

his sister drew near.

It was enough to cause Ailís to pick up the pace. "What's wrong?" she whispered, panic coloring her words.

"Nothing," Camaráin said. "Just thought it'd be easier to talk if I looked like something happened."

Ailís smiled and threw her arm around her brother's shoulder to play up the act. "You're far cleverer than I give you credit for."

"Compared to you, I'm always clever."

She scoffed. "You're lucky I can't shout at you for that."

"Why do you think I said it here?" Camaráin allowed a grin to flash before returning to the expression of false concern.

"Brat," Ailís muttered, but then eyed the movement in her brother's bag. "Why'd you bring him here?"

"I think he was looking for you. Ma kept almost stepping on him. I think he was doing it on purpose after a while."

"He's taking after us already. I guess it's a good sign she hasn't thrown him out a window yet, right?"

"I...took him with me before she got the idea."

"Good lad." Ailís stifled a chuckle.

Camaráin nodded and gestured to the door with his head. "So, wanna get out of here? I guess I got here at the right time."

"Oh, *yes* please."

"*Ahem*," sounded a loud voice from behind. The tension in the room returned as Miss Róisín approached. "Ailís. Are you done convincing your brother to leave? *Some* of us care about the performance tomorrow."

"Not me," Ailís muttered under her breath, even if she would be forced to take part in it. Regardless, the opportunity to leave was too much to pass up. She pouted at her brother and fluttered her eyes—their code for their often-foolproof plan of "cry to get out of doing things"—and forced the tears to stream down her cheeks as she turned around. Looking at the dark void of Miss Róisín's eyes through the watery blur, she began to sputter, "M-M-Miss Róisín...it's...it's our Ma. Sh-sh-she...she just..."

Miss Róisín held up a hand to quiet her, and said, "Go. Whatever you need, just go." It was difficult to tell whether her words were of genuine concern or if she just wanted Ailís to leave. Her face did not change one way or the other—nor did it ever seem to. There was a rumor that when she was born, the doctor cried for how angry she looked. No one dared to ask, of course.

But, regardless of the intent, Ailís still managed a gracious smile. "Th-thank you, ma'am," she said as she turned toward the door.

"Tomorrow, though!" the instructor called. "Don't you forget, you're front and center."

Okay, so she *did* only want Ailís to leave.

The freedom of breathing fresh air—that wonderful aroma of manure and out-of-date fish—was invigorating just the same. The horror of performing the dance incorrectly and facing Miss Róisín's wrath was a problem for tomorrow. For now, Ailís was content to kick off her ghillies and let her toes work their way through the mud.

While, on the whole, her brother was a know-it-all who liked to push her buttons, every once in a while he managed to be useful. So, Ailís tussled his mop of hair to the point of complaint as a show of gratitude, which was the custom at the time—or so she claimed. (Still unclear.)

When they traveled far enough away from the dance hall for Ailís not to fear the instructor chasing after her, she inched closer to Camaráin's bag and peered inside. Pilib was resting contentedly, but when he noticed the light peering through and Ailís's face, he opened his mouth once again in his approximation of a smile. It made Ailís's heart swell.

"So, little brother," she said with happiness enriching her voice. "Where shall we go?"

Camaráin gestured to his bag. "With him? Probably just home?"

Ailís snapped her fingers and pointed at him in acknowledgment. "Right. Back to convincing Ma to let us keep him."

"She's just going to go back to saying we need to get rid of him the moment we come home."

Looking down at her muddy feet, Ailís said, "Not if we keep her too distracted!"

"At this rate, she's going to get rid of you before him." Camaráin shook his head and made for home, a grin on his face, perhaps amused at the joke, or perhaps imagining life as an only child.

Regardless of the reasoning, Ailís still returned the grin in kind. With hands on her hips, she whispered, "As long as I can take him with me wherever I end up." She skipped after her brother, mud splashing on her feet and up her legs.

(Her poor mother.)

Liam's head still pounded, and not just from the fall the day before.

Lord Saibhir did not take too kindly to the missing delivery, and he ensured Liam would have the marks to prove it for some time.

He had the right to be angry, to be sure. Liam was plenty angry himself. But to confiscate his horses from him as a punishment? It was not only cruel—Liam's livelihood was tied to those horses, as were a couple things of his that were literally tied to those horses—but it was also perplexing. Nóran horses were unpleasant; it wouldn't be long before Lord Saibhir was tracking him down and *begging* to return them because they wanted to assert their own self-importance one way or another. There was nothing for Liam but to walk back to Baile, all pride gone, and sit in a puddle of mud by the markets, and hope for someone to take pity upon him and give him free food.

It was unfortunate, though, that the morning markets were just that—the *morning* markets, not the mid-afternoon markets. The stalls were empty, and so, too, were people's capacities for generosity.

He frowned, his stomach rumbling, and not a penny in his pocket, left with nothing to do but sit and watch the people walk on by and pay him no mind as though he didn't exist. Folk with coin purses jingling or full loaves of bread in their hands, laughter filling the air around them. Liam studied their faces, intent on remembering each target of his discontent, though they were all faces of people he had never known.

One face, however, did catch his eye. The familiar face of a young girl, probably no older than ten or eleven years, walking barefoot beside a boy younger than she, perhaps her brother.

Where he recognized her from, he could not tell. But it nagged at him for the rest of the day more than his empty pockets and emptier stomach.

Chapter Seven

True to her word, Miss Róisín forced Ailís to the front of the pack when the recital began the next day. For a variety of reasons, Ailís had cause to be nervous. One, she was prone to spells of stage fright when faced with large crowds. Two, the issue of Pilib's placement in the house still had not been resolved (Ma had been otherwise distracted by the mysterious appearance of muddy footsteps on the floor, walls, and somehow the ceiling).

Three—and most importantly—Ailís had no idea of what the routine was. She was never sent notes for those practices she missed due to undisclosed circumstances (such as pretending to go and not disclosing to her ma that she had not).

All the girls were lining up in their appointed places—from the most skillful in the front to the infirmed and otherwise unskilled dancers in the back. It had been Ailís's hope to remain at the rear, next to the girl with the club foot, but such was not the case. When she had arrived at the dance hall with her ma and brother, Miss Róisín did not say a word to her.

But she smiled. And that never meant anything good. Ailís resigned herself to her fate.

From the other side of the curtain, the sound of the gathering crowd grew louder. When Miss Róisín's head was turned, Ailís managed to sneak a peek through the curtain, and by her estimation, almost the entire village of Baile had gathered. Ma and Camaráin sat at a bench on the far right side, her brother having placed his bag on his lap. She could see nothing moving within, but she knew that Pilib was inside. Ma was surprisingly amenable to bringing the dragon along, though it was probably more due to wishing not to have the house ransacked by the Inquisition should Pilib's presence have become known and they were not at home, than it was an acceptance of Pilib.

It was a small step, anyway.

Before Ailís could examine the crowd any further, Miss Róisín's talons dug into her shoulder and jerked her backward, placing her back in her starting position. Those dark pools filled Róisín's eyes again, and whatever dark magic was within them held Ailís in place with no inclination to move. Ailís couldn't help but wonder why the Inquisition paid no heed to Miss Róisín while they exhausted their efforts on dragons, but that was a mystery that not even Uncle Iósaf had spoken on—probably due to his fear of the dance instructor, as well.

A fuller complement of musicians was lining up to the side, including two additional fiddlers, a piper, a tin whistler, and an extra percussionist. The final adjustments were made to their respective instruments, a prelude to judgment day for Ailís. The pit in her stomach only grew larger and larger. A small part of her prayed for any delay to the recital, any distraction that would allow her to shuffle three or four rows backward and away from Miss Róisín's eyes. It would take a miracle.

The musicians nodded to Miss Róisín and she responded in kind, flashing one last horrifying glance at the dancers. Everyone went still, all paralyzed in place by the instructor's glare. The instructor disappeared to the other side of the curtain, and the loud din quieted. A truly wicked talent. Part of Ailís wanted to learn that power. It needed to be shared with the world!

Ailís clenched her hands into fists to prevent them from trembling. The seconds were counting down. All that remained was the introductory speech on the part of the instructor, and then she could finally get this over with.

Until she looked up and the curtain had already fallen. Whether for spite or wanting to get the show on the road, Miss Róisín elected *not* to give the customary speech. The fumbling of instruments off to the side indicated to Ailís that it had been neither planned nor discussed with them, but it at least afforded her the extra moments to collect herself and survey the gathered crowd and ignore that vicious glare the instructor had directed her way.

A small smattering of applause trickled through the crowd. Ailís looked to her right and saw Ma and Camaráin smiling and clapping. It was the first time in days she had not seen irritation on Ma's face, which was a plus. Elsewhere in the crowd sat people Ailís was familiar with, folk she had often walked past on trips to and from the morning markets or the schoolhouse. Lined in the back were a handful of Inquisitors, including the one who had visited the house the day before. Or at least Ailís assumed it was the same man; his face was obscured by a long beam that only he could have been tall enough to stand behind.

Closing her eyes, Ailís collected her thoughts, readied herself for those first notes, hoping that whatever proceeded would not bequeath upon her an evil dance instructor's wrath later. The fumbling and rustling to the side ceased, a hush fell over the crowd, eager anticipation gripping them all, and a trail of sweat trickled down the small of Ailís's back. She heard whispering among the musicians, a confirmation shared from person to person.

"A-one, a-two," she heard, the words thumping in rhythm with the bodhrans. "A-one, two, three—"

Ailís opened her eyes, lifting her right foot off the ground in anticipation. Everyone else lifted their left.

"Wait, that's her!" a voice called from the back just as the fiddler brought the bow to the strings for the first note, only to stop. Several feet stumbled behind Ailís, and at least one person fell.

Miss Róisín appeared out of nowhere as if summoned by the shadows. Her head shot from left to right like a bird of prey hunting her quarry, and a man caked in mud emerged from the throng, pointing an accusatory finger to the stage.

"Sir, return to your seat for the duration of the performance," the instructor commanded, the shards of ice in her voice understood to all the villagers.

But this man didn't appear to be from Baile. Else he would have returned to his seat and probably would have already been scared to tears. No, he ignored Miss Róisín's demand and continued to approach, his arm not dropping to his side. His eyes locked with Ailís's, ignoring the dance instructor entirely. He looked oddly familiar.

"You, there!" Miss Róisin pointed at the Inquisitors in the back. "Make yourselves useful for once and get him out of here!"

The Inquisitors responded with a clank of ill-fitting armor and rushed proclamations of "Yes, ma'am," pushing their way forward.

The muddy man kept approaching the stage, his finger trained on Ailís. "You! You stole those eggs from me!"

Ailís turned over her shoulder, wondering if someone taller had perhaps been behind her. She then remembered that she was the tallest girl in the group (only by an inch or two, but still).

"No, I mean *you*, girl!" the man asserted, brushing off hands grasping at his shoulder. "You stole those dragon eggs from me!"

An inclination to tremble gripped Ailís, but she stood her ground, even as the entire gathering glared at her. In her periphery, she could see Camaráin holding his messenger bag and her Ma rising to her feet. A cool sensation traveled up the length of her arms as the man drew closer and closer. Beneath the layer of mud masking his face, she finally recognized him: the merchant whose wagon she broke. The merchant from whom she had rescued Pilib.

Why he was accusing her of theft of *multiple* eggs, though, perplexed her. Was there another egg elsewhere? She only found the one.

"What, nothing to say for yourself, you little thief?" the man growled.

"I didn't steal anything from you," Ailís managed to squeak. She took two steps backward, bumping into the row of girls behind her. Protective hands wrapped around her shoulders.

"Convincing display. Why're you trying to run, then?"

"Because you're frightening the girl, you fool!" Ailís did not expect the rebuke to come from the mouth of Miss Róisín, but it did. It felt like a strange dream. She was expecting it to end with the instructor lulling her into a false sense of security only to eat her whole in the next breath. Judging from the crowd, most were expecting the same.

"But she stole my dragon eggs *and* my livelihood!" the merchant exclaimed.

He seemed to have forgotten the Inquisitors were present. The tall Inquisitor, Eamon, crossed his arms, his face still managing to be obscured by the wooden beams above. "Your dragon eggs, you say?"

"*And* my livelihood! Return both to me, girl!"

"I am certain it's not within the girl's power to offer the latter, but perhaps we should discuss the former."

The merchant sneered. "We have nothing to discuss and you have no jurisdiction over me. I want my eggs back!"

"You mean *my* eggs, churl!" a voice boomed over the crowd.

All attention shot toward the back of the gathering—save for that of the merchant, who stared at the ground below and shuddered in place. A portly man in garish clothing thumped forward, flanked on either side by what passed for guards. Ailís recognized their faces as being from Baile, but it had been some time since she saw them last. The man they stood beside looked out of place, even standing amidst a gaggle of Inquisitors who had cornered the market on looking out of place.

"You would do well to hand over my eggs, girl," the man commanded. "They rightly belong to me."

Before Ailís could defend herself—or even question where there was ever another egg— Eamon turned around, his head finally unobscured by the beam, but his face still a mystery. "Your desire for such draconic contraband is alarming, Saibhir," the Inquisitor said. "Need we have a conversation with High

Inquisitor Dónal about this?"

"Silence, false knight!" Saibhir exclaimed, his chins jiggling. He shot a vengeful glare at the merchant. "And you! Such vile indiscretion! What fool are you to proclaim to all that you carried *dragon eggs* on your person? These charlatans would descend upon you in an instant!"

"*You* speak to *me* about indiscretion?" the merchant responded. "It's *you* who has set the Inquisition upon this village! If anyone should be descended upon, it is you!"

One of the Inquisitors accompanying Eamon held up a finger, pointing at both parties. "One moment, if you would. Who need we descend upon?" Part of his pauldron fell off as he pointed, and with it, the rest of the armor on that arm.

"Him!" the merchant and Saibhir shouted, both pointing accusatory fingers at one another.

Eamon sighed and placed his hands on his hips, "Nuts to this, just take them both in. Us 'charlatans' can leave it to the High Inquisitor to find out."

Saibhir puffed out his chest—and stomach, and chin, and other chin—and yelled, "You shan't have the chance. Guards!"

In response, his guards jumped forward, all too eager and all too clumsy. The one on the left grasped at the hilt tied to his waist, which elicited a startled shout from the crowd. Then everyone realized there was no steel attached to it. He turned to his comrade and stated plainly what could have remained a whisper, "Do you still have the other half of this?"

The second guard carefully unwrapped his sword belt and tipped the scabbard upside down, then shook it, a frown growing on his face the longer the attempts continued. There was enough of a rattling inside to indicate there *was* steel inside, at least.

The struggle persisted, and the first impatient guard opted throw the bladeless hilt at Eamon's head. He didn't throw quite high enough, and it instead clanked against the Inquisitor's cuirass.

Then the startled shouts persisted. Ailís was tossed about as her fellow dancers dispersed. The crowd screamed and fanned out in all directions, running away from the looming fight. Her instinct being to follow the will of the crowd, Ailís glanced in the direction of where her family had been seated, only to not see them there anymore. She turned, finding the crowd running every which way, including into the middle of the impending fray between Saibhir's guards and the Inquisitors, only delaying it further as each party readied their strikes, only to halt them, wait for people to pass, and tap their feet in impatient frustration.

It was only in this momentary distraction that Ailís felt a firm arm wrap around her chest and drag her backward. She screamed in defiance, swatting at the arm, fearful tears streaming down her face.

When next she opened her eyes, she was past the reach of the stage, held tightly by her ma. "Are you okay, my sweet girl?" Ma said, holding Ailís's face in her hands, wiping away the tears with her thumbs.

Ailís shook in Ma's embrace but managed a nod. She looked past Ma's shoulder to see Camaráin clutching his bag by the straps, Pilib's curious head poking out once more.

"Good." Ma looked over her shoulder, the chaos of the abandoned slip-jig not yet having reached the alleyway they had crouched in. "You're sure you only took *one* egg from this man?"

Her eyes flaring, Ailís said, "Do you really think I'd still be hiding it at this point?"

Ma grunted noncommittally, still seeming unconvinced. "Fine. Back to the house. Now. Then pack your bags—there's no safety for us here." Before Ailís could question it, Ma turned on her heels and ran, dragging both kids by the arms.

"Ma!" Ailís called, nearly stumbling over her own feet, ripping her arm free so she could maintain her balance as she followed. "What do you mean, 'pack our bags?' Where are we going?"

They reached the end of the alleyway and stopped, Ma peering around the corner before gesturing them along.

"Whether or not the Inquisitors believe there's a dragon in our house is irrelevant. The accusation has been made." The house drew nearer, still in perfect condition. That much was a relief, at least. "You want your dragon, Ailís? Then this is the reality of it."

Ailís's breath ran ragged in her throat and she had to slow her pace, matched by her brother who struggled just the same. She held Camaráin's hand and followed Ma as best as she could. "But where are we going?" she asked, her words halted while she caught her breath.

They reached the door to the house and shuffled inside, Ma barring it shut behind them. "To the only person who understands that reality of indulging in the pursuit of dragons. The only person who will know what to do with Pilib." She pushed past the children and walked toward her bedroom before looking over her shoulder and stating plainly:

"Your uncle Iósaf."

Chapter Eight

Had Ailís been holding something, she'd have dropped it. To illustrate the point, she took off her ghillies, held them, and then dropped them. She stared at her ma, uncertain she had heard correctly. When she peered at Camaráin, he had much the same reaction. Pilib even jumped out of the bag to mime a shocked face.

Either they had heard wrong, or Ma had misspoken. One way or the other, there was simply no way...

"What?" Ma said, standing at the threshold to her room. "Go on, pack up your things. We can't dawdle."

Ailís opened her mouth, but for once, only incoherent sounds came out.

"Did you really say, 'Uncle Iósaf?'" Camaráin asked.

"Yes," Ma said, far blunter than she probably intended. "What's wrong? For how much you talk about 'Uncle Iósaf' this and 'Uncle Iósaf' that, I thought you'd jump at the chance to see him."

The weight of the statement threatened to trample Ailís. She looked at her brother, who likely viewed their uncle as more a myth than anything else. After all, Camaráin had only been a year old when Uncle Iósaf disappeared. For Ailís, the reality was something greater. He was someone who regaled her with heroic stories of the great dragons of Nóra when he put her to bed rather than the tales that had been approved under the watchful eye of the Inquisition. Whenever he'd read something from a book titled *The Grand Blessings of Blessedon the Blessed: An Exercise in Nominative Determinism*, he'd swear Ailís to secrecy and put her to bed next to a copy of *The Inquisition and You: Basic Mathematics for a Smarter Age* to keep up appearances for her mother's sake (though he did eventually cross out "Smarter" and scribbled "Dumber" under it). Ma never did question why he read Ailís a math book every night, but maybe she knew better.

And if she was offering to take the children to see their uncle, she must have known a *lot* better.

Halted by hesitation, Ailís managed a brief nod. "Then...you know where he is? He's...okay?"

Ma scoffed, shaking her head. "Your uncle has been living in the woods for the last six years. As far as I know, he loves it."

"*What?!*" Ailís's eyes flared with disbelief. She narrowed the gap between herself and her ma, Pilib squawking with fright as she zipped on by. "You've known where he was all this time and you didn't say anything?"

"I did. And now you know, too. Go on."

"But why didn't you...just say he was okay?"

Frowning, Ma retreated into her bedroom and drew a bag out from beneath her bed. As she let it thud atop the bed with a huff, she ran a hand through her tangled hair and said, "It'd have hurt you more to know he was still out there and well, but unable to be with you. You may not understand now...but one day you will."

"How would you know that?" Ailís grumbled beneath her breath—or what passed for it by her standards. It was still a normal speaking volume.

"Because it's something *I* understand all too well." Something flashed in Ma's eyes that Ailís hadn't seen in ages: sadness. Raw, genuine sadness. "I haven't seen my brother in six years. Six years that I could have depended on him had he not decided that his fanciful interests were greater than the safety of our family, but I've instead been given six years of feeling anger and pain toward him. It's not simply his insistence on learning the truth about the history of the dragons and our land rather than accepting the Inquisition's lies. It's that the brother he was, the man who stopped at nothing to ensure you two were well cared-for after Camaráin was born and I was left alone...he has been long gone. Whoever the man is in the woods...he's not the same one I knew." A tear trickled down Ma's cheek as she packed her bag, a heavy silence lingering in the air between her and Ailís.

For her part, Ailís could only stand and listen...but something had gripped her and kept a hold on her attention. "You said...'the Inquisition's lies?'"

Ma stopped packing and turned to face her daughter, the tear on her cheek drying. A tuft of steam could have wisped along for how red-hot her face grew. "Oh, for the love of..." Another frustrated sigh escaped her. "Just pack your damn bag, Ailís."

The sound of Pilib's scales scraping against the floor as he slithered over perhaps only exacerbated the situation, but Ailís was happy to feel him climb up her leg and back until he perched atop her shoulder. She scratched behind his head, the hatchling responding with a delighted trill. Ma had resumed packing her things, but the tension of the moment was not lost on Ailís. "Will you still be happy to see him?" she asked.

The question hung suspended between them for a long moment. Ma pressed her hands onto her bed and looked down, pondering the question for too long. "That's not an easy answer."

"It's an easy question, though."

"For you, perhaps." The threads of the blanket on Ma's bed wore against her bunched fingers, holding on for dear life. "I'll not ask again. Get packing, the both of you."

Ailís didn't press her further and did as she was told, staring at Camaráin as she passed him. "Did you hear that?" she asked in a sharp, excited whisper, by her standards. It was still a normal speaking volume. "Uncle Iósaf's stories were all—"

"Take the hint, Ailís," Camaráin answered, shuffling over to his room perhaps a bit too expeditiously. It appeared as though he was looking over his shoulder before skirting inside. Strange, but he was a strange lad.

Before Ailís could pass the threshold of her room, Pilib began to grumble, and a cold chill ran down the length of her arm. She looked over her shoulder and noticed the dragon's attention had been focused the door. "What is it?" she asked.

The loud rapping at the door interrupted her before she could finish the question. She gulped, a pit forming in her stomach.

Ma rushed out of her room, more frustration apparent than there had been the day before. "Get in your room," she said.

"Ma, I—"

"*Now*, Ailís."

Pilib obeyed before Ailís and jumped off her shoulder, scampering around the corner. By the time Ailís had followed suit, the front door had been thrust open, and the Inquisitor standing at the door—and beyond her view, naturally—was Eamon. Beside him was the Inquisitor who had questioned Ailís the other day while she went to collect berries and flowers.

"What, Eamon?" Ma demanded. There was no effort to hide the hostility in her voice.

Eamon crossed his arms, as he always seemed to do. "You seem rattled, Máirín. In a rush?"

"And you seem as though you should be elsewhere. That brawl at the recital only happened ten minutes ago. Shouldn't you be...handling that, or something?"

"Shift change," Eamon said with a shrug. "One of my comrades took over."

"Took over...your spot in a brawl, then."

"Admittedly, no one was really fighting. It's been one long argument over who is at fault for those eggs."

Ailís narrowed her eyes. "But there's only one," she muttered to herself, staring at Pilib's curious face.

"So, someone is being yelled at in your place," Ma said.

"That's about the size of it, yes," Eamon affirmed.

"And that is continuing to happen rather than them being taken in for questioning."

"Well, as it were, we...cannot take them in as such since neither of them..."

"Yes, yes, neither has the eggs on their person, your jurisdiction is a farce, blah, blah, blah. We've been over this already."

"Our jurisdiction is important, Máirín," Eamon asserted.

There was offence in his tone. If only Ailís could see equivalent reaction on his face. "The duties of our order are imperative to keeping the peace throughout Nóra."

Ma paused and raised a finger, pointing to the commotion further in the village. No words were discernible, but the aggressive tone of the noise was all the confirmation she needed. "You're doing a great job. Now, why are you here, Eamon?"

"Well, we would be remiss in our duties if we did not follow up on these claims that your daughter...stole these dragon eggs, was it?"

"I can tell by your tone you also find it ridiculous that Ailís could have done such a thing."

"Stranger things have happened. My cousin was chased by a goat last summer."

"How is *that* stranger?"

Eamon grew quiet, his long and thick arms falling to his side, his hands gesturing as though to illustrate his point. When that failed, he said, "Well, anyway. We're just here to do our due diligence, Máirín. And seeing as you're presently..." His large frame tilted to the left and Ailís feared he was about to fall and knock the house down. "...packing to go somewhere, it seems? Some ten minutes after your daughter was accused of harboring draconic contraband? I would say we are within our rights to be curious."

Ma crossed her arms. "Well, I am within my rights to demand you present a writ of investigation."

"Present a what now?" Eamon sounded genuinely confused.

"You heard me."

"No, no, sorry. I mean...present a what? A writ of investigation?"

Ma nodded.

"I...I admit I..." The Inquisitor's voice drew lower and lower to the point of a whisper. He turned to his partner and murmured—though still quite loudly, for his deep voice practically vibrated off the beams of the house—with a shred of embarrassment, "Have you heard of a 'writ of investigation?'"

The second Inquisitor shook his head. "I never have," he said.

With her hands on her hips, Ma leaned over and asked, with all manner of spite coloring her tongue, "Well, how many times have you needed to search someone's home for quote-unquote draconic contraband?"

The Inquisitors both sputtered and strung together a stream of nonsense before simultaneously stating, "None, ma'am."

"Well, it's very much a thing you need here. That's definitely the way it's always been."

Ailís inclined her head as she listened to her ma. Her words were growing...less convincing.

Well, to her. These Inquisitors were...well...

"I suppose we need to consult Lord Saibhir on the matter, then," the second Inquisitor stated.

Eamon outturned his hands. "Lord Saibhir may not be inclined to grant us anything at the moment..."

"Hmph, what a shame," Ma said, one hand already on the door. "Apologies, but you'll have to wait until you have that writ in hand and signed by Lord Saibhir himself. Good day, gentlemen." Questions began to escape Eamon before the door slammed in his face.

A disappointed groan rumbled on the other side of the door.

Ailís raised her eyebrows as Ma walked back to her bedroom

with a sly smile. She was even chuckling. Before she disappeared from view, Ma motioned Ailís back into her room with her hand, and that was that.

When Ailís at last walked into her bedroom, Pilib was pulling an empty bag to the center of the room with his teeth. He hopped into the bag, his part in assisting evidently having been accomplished.

Though she was not a habitual gambler—largely because she was only eleven years old—Ailís would have felt confident just then to bet that stranger things had *not* happened.

Chapter Nine

Enough time had passed that not only did the family have ample opportunity to pack the bare necessities, but they were also afforded the chance to stow away extra food for the northbound journey to the woods.

When Ailís noticed her ma loading food storage bins, a wave of concern ran through her. "Ma," she had said, "what about when the Inquisitors return with that writ of investigation? We should leave while we still have time!"

Ma only smiled at that rebuke, the multiple times the concern had been raised. By the time they left the house, her head was held high, worry long since departed from her expression.

Ailís followed her, Camaráin not far behind. Though she had been concerned about packing lighter to ensure Pilib maintained some manner of comfort in her bag, she wound up with plenty of room to spare. There was not much to be done when many of her clothes were still in need of a wash after being coated in mud. And after the hatchling rustled about inside the bag for the first few steps, he seemed to have fashioned himself a comfortable bed and fallen asleep.

She looked over her shoulder at her brother, who was lagging behind somewhat, but at least did not seem wearied.

There was some heft to his bag for whatever reason, but he was resistant to anyone carrying it around for him. He had been acting strange lately (well, strang*er*, at any rate) but kept to himself regardless. As long as he wasn't causing trouble, whatever else he was hiding was an afterthought.

The end of the village loomed ahead, the final row of houses standing tall as a reminder of the smaller stature of the family's own home, and the wonderful scent of fresh wildflowers and enchanting meadows were enough of a lure for Ailís to pick up her pace and file in beside her ma. It was strange the way the enchanting aromas stopped by the time they reached Baile, as though the breeze would carry them in its arms, only to fumble it at the first sight of mud, muck, and Inquisitors. It even seemed the meadows themselves would take one glance at Baile and think, "Nah," and go about their business elsewhere.

In the distance, the argument between Lord Saibhir and the Inquisition echoed over the horizon with a strength unheard of since the Great Potato Chicanery of three years past (a truly deplorable day responsible for the loss of one angry man's mind and nearly twice as many potatoes). Ailís couldn't help but be impressed at how long an argument could endure before it resorted to blows, but another Uncle Iósaf staple reminded her, "That's just politics, kiddo."

She allowed herself to breathe a sigh of relief when the mud became soft and verdant grass. The breeze was gentle, the air was crisp, the stench of manure was fleeting, and the clink-clank of ill-fitting armor was approaching.

Wait, that last part wasn't good.

An annoyed tut-tut-tut sounded behind her and Ailís suddenly found herself bunched behind her ma alongside Camaráin. She could see a muscular metal frame form behind Ma, but no face otherwise.

Ma stiffened her shoulders and puffed her chin out. "Were you able to obtain that writ of investigation, then?" she asked.

An armored foot kicked rocks off to the side. "No," a voice said—Eamon's, from the sound of it. Disappointment filled his words.

Beside him stood the other Inquisitor who had visited the house earlier, still as out-of-place as he had always been. There was a fresh brown splash across his cuirass that blocked the sigil of the Inquisition.

It didn't go unnoticed. "Not for lack of trying?"

The second Inquisitor hung his head and murmured, "I walked toward the commotion and Lord Saibhir threw...this at me." He gestured to his chest. "I...pray it is only mud."

"It's not," Eamon whispered, just loud enough for everyone to hear.

"I know," the second man admitted.

"Hmph, well," Ma interjected, pushing the children back a handful of steps. "If that's all, gentlemen, we will just be—"

"No, Máirín, you know it's not." Disappointment, silent accusation, and frustration were apparent in Eamon's voice. "I wasn't wrong to assume you were in a rush to be elsewhere."

"And what's your point, Eamon?"

Eamon spread his gauntleted hands toward Ma, fingers outstretched. "Might I ask where you're off to?"

"No, you may not." She grasped Ailís and Camaráin's shoulders and turned them around to face north again. "Come along, children."

"Hold, Máirín." Eamon took a loud, metallic step forward. "I asked you a—"

"Do you have a writ of questioning, Eamon?" Ma asked pointedly, not bothering to turn around.

The Inquisitor stopped in his place. "A writ of what?"

"Just as I've said. A writ of questioning."

"And such a writ is...?"

Ma grunted. "Necessary for you to obtain if you wish to ask me any questions I am otherwise under no obligation to answer. It is well within my rights to demand."

Ailís turned around to see Eamon lean over to his comrade, though his face was blocked by the other man's pauldron. "Is that correct?" he asked.

The second Inquisitor shrugged, placing a hand on Eamon's shoulder. "If we also need to obtain a writ of searching from Lord Saibhir...I guess it would stand to reason?"

"My god, have we been breaking the law all these years?"

"I don't know," the nameless Inquisitor murmured, his face pale. "I shudder to think what the High Inquisitor will do to us if we have been."

"Yes, well." Ma cleared her throat and shoved the children forward. "As you were, gentlemen. Goodbye." The Inquisitors did not follow.

After several minutes in silence—save for pained winces as both children protested against being dragged along by the scruffs of their necks—Ailís looked up at her ma and asked, "How did you learn to stop the Inquisitors so easily?"

"It comes with the experience of teaching children. And at the end of the day, what are the Inquisitors but larger, dumber children?"

Ailís laughed. "I never knew this side of you existed, Ma."

"Where do you think my brother got it from?" she muttered.

"I have a question," Camaráin said, adjusting the shoulder strap of his bag, its contents thumping against his hip. "You ask us questions all the time but you never give us a writ of questioning from Lord Saibhir."

Ma raised her eyebrows. "Oh, I ask questions *all* the time, do I?"

Camaráin backed away, but said, "Well, like when we came home with the dragon egg..." He trailed off, his eyes widening for some strange reason, his mind seeming to travel elsewhere. After a second's hesitation, he said, "Yeah, the dragon egg. You could have given us one when Pilib hatched, but..."

"Would you believe that a parent is under no obligation to present such a writ to their children?"

"That seems an abuse of power," Camaráin said.

A hearty laugh burst from Ma.

Ailís hadn't heard her ma laugh like that in years. It seemed some great weight had been lifted from her. "Or is it just that you lied about those writs?" she asked.

Ma smiled again and clapped her hands on the children's shoulders. "You may both drive me to my wit's end sometimes, but I'm proud to have raised such intelligent, observant kids." She looked at Camaráin, whose eyes had widened with shock, to which she responded, "Yes, yes, I know. Sometimes I have to lie. It's not my fault if they believe it."

"So," Ailís said, stifling a chuckle, "everything you said about the writs of questioning and investigation..."

Ma nodded. "There's no such thing. The Inquisitors are just idiots."

The rest of the day's walk passed with similar mirth.

Chapter Ten

D reams came easily that night. They often did when one walked more in one day than they had in their entire life (or so Ailís and Camaráin persistently repeated, as though they were not notorious for running themselves ragged and running their ma insane, but the point still remained).

When daylight waned and a grove loomed ahead, the family took the opportunity to rest their weary bodies and continue the journey to the woods the following day. Mist-dampened fields of green had never been so comfortable. At least, it was easy to feel that way when accustomed to the "sleeping on the ground" options being either mud or "please let this be mud."

From the moment Ailís rested her head on the soft earth, crickets chirping their nocturnal soliloquy, she was at peace. Her family lay beside her—and not only her ma and brother. Pilib emerged from her bag to nestle up in the crook of her arms, his cold scales still providing a gentle warmth. A lurch into the depths of her dreams was all too inevitable once Ailís closed her eyes.

In her dream, she soared through the sky again, the wind as much a part of her as her eyes and nose. The sensation of weightlessness was unlike anything she had experienced, just as the expansive panorama before her challenged her to find any sight more stunning. Mountains crested the horizon, snowcaps glittering against a sunlight the radiance of which she had never beheld. The air rippled as she turned her head to see she once again had wings, beautiful silver wings to match the scales of her long serpentine body. The skies were hers to command, the world within reach, so long as she had the desire to see it all.

The ocean shimmered below and she dove like a gull seizing its aquatic prey, chasing the golden light that expanded along its length. She laughed as the shockwave of air pressed against her, her stomach lurching, her heart pounding in double succession as though a second heart beat in concert with hers. The water drew ever nearer, her voice echoing across the earth, droplets of water splashing up to greet her, gentle waves crashing in accordance with the will of the tides. And when she leveled in time to skirt the face of the ocean, her toes cutting currents in their wake, the rush of salt air assaulted her senses.

She felt it for the first time, yet it was a sensation all too familiar. It was a memory of which she had no recollection, but something urged her forward to the gilded sun looming in the distance.

What it meant, Ailís did not know. But she wanted to know. She wanted to discover what lay beyond the golden horizon. She knew not why it was hers to discover...but she was compelled to learn, nonetheless.

The mountains were her destination—of that, and of little else, she was certain. With an excited smile, she batted her wings against the ocean and ascended, her body gliding along the wind's wisps, unimpeded. Faster she flew, the world cracking with each flap of her wings.

She expected the thunderous echoes of her flight to quell when she allowed herself to soar along the currents of the air...but even as she furled her wings back, the loud cracks continued independent of her.

An unfamiliar voice nagged at her. *"Wake up,"* it said. *"You need to wake up."*

Ailís winced as a strong force pulled her away from the mountains. Her body shook, something sharp digging into her shoulders. The world darkened around her as pitch black clouds loomed overhead. Her wings took on a mind of their own, diverting her further away from her original destination and back toward the Nóran landscapes to which she was accustomed. Her heart thumped its soft rhythm, as did a louder beat that was not her own.

She wanted so desperately to continue to fly, but something—or some*one*—demanded her attention. Another pointed jolt jabbed at her chest, and a commanding and high voice echoed once more in her ears:

"Wake up."

Ailís opened her eyes, moonlight having long since enshrouded the grove. A rasped yet high-pitched growl resounded nearby, and she noticed Pilib was no longer resting in her arms. She pushed herself up to a seated position, groaning against a dull ache in her shoulder and chest. The threads of her shirt had been torn by what appeared to be small claws. As she narrowed her eyes, she saw the dragon positioned in front of her, his small legs entrenched in the ground, baring his tiny teeth at the shadows ahead.

"Pilib!" she commanded in a sharp whisper. "Quiet! You're

gonna wake Ma and Cam up!"

But Pilib paid the command no mind. A faint tingle sent a chill up Ailís's arm as she watched the shadows coalesce into something validating the dragon's threat assessment. Two men emerged from the darkness, short and stout, the both of them, the one on the left with a hooked nose while the one on the right had a hooked hand, a hooked nose, and the unfortunate appearance of a hook. They both strode forward, Pilib seeming to be caught between wanting to charge at them and wanting to back away in fright.

Ailís found herself in much the same manner. "Who are you?" she asked, her voice trembling.

The hook-nosed (and only hook-nosed) man stopped and smiled, exposing a row of crooked, rotting teeth. "S'pose oughtta ask that o' you, don't I?" He chuckled, folding his fingers across his portly belly. "Ain't seen you lot 'round here, now have I?"

"In this specific field? Probably not," Ailís replied. "I don't know why you'd see anyone here. There's nothing around."

"See folk 'round her plenty, I do. Just they know better'n to...stay 'round here, if you catch my meaning."

Ailís shook her head. "I don't."

"Ah, well, you're young yet. Lessons to be taught tonight, is all."

Hook-man took an awkward step forward—the difficulties of basically being shaped like a hook and all—and said, "Right, then. Bags, empty 'em. We'll be takin' em."

"What?" Ailís raised an eyebrow. "Why? No. This is our stuff."

"Right..." Hook-man said, scratching his hook-head with his

hook-hand. "And now it's ours."

"That's not how that works," Ailís asserted, Pilib continuing to growl in front of her.

The solely hook-nosed man furrowed his normal-shaped brow and said, "Think we know what thievin' entails, little lady. We been at it a long while. Now come on, don't need to make this too—and can you quiet your dog already? I'm tryin' to educate you here."

"My dog? Pilib's not a—oops." Ailís clasped her hand over her mouth, but it was too late. Pilib's growls and squawks grew louder, though hardly with any menace.

"Yeah, that ain't any dog I've ever seen, mate," Hook-man said. "Kinda ugly for one, doncha think?"

"Hey!" Ailís shouted in a show of offense.

"Well, he is! Looks more like a big lizard or a dragon than a—sweet mercy, that's a dragon, ain't it?!" Hook-man froze in place, the loud clank of something falling out of his back pocket shaking the ground. An expression of pure shock remained on his face.

"Hoo-hoo!" Hook-nose-and-only-hook-nose exclaimed. "This's far better'n any ol' shakedown!"

Ailís reached forward and drew Pilib close. "You're with the Inquisition, aren't you? Well, you're gonna need to show me a writ of...of...well, you know!" Of all the times to forget the thing she was supposed to be lying about.

It did no good. The thieves looked at her and laughed. "Girl, if we was with the Inquisition, I don't think we'd be doin' this sorta thing on the regular," Hook-man said. "Kind o' you to think so highly of us, though."

The thief formerly and presently known as Hook-nose took

a step forward, cracking his knuckles. "Best we don't make this more difficult than you've already made it. We'll be takin' the dragon off yer hands."

Ailís reached for a nearby rock and threw. "Get away!" she yelled, releasing the rock with more force than she thought possible, her arm hardly feeling the tension of the air as it whipped through.

The span of a second heard first a whistle, then a clunk. The hook-nosed thief's head lurched backward, then his body followed suit, and then he became acquainted with the ground. He didn't move.

"Hey!" Hook-man shouted, sparing his partner a quick glance before stepping forward.

Pilib growled as the thief approached, and a cold surge flowed through Ailís's arm. Again, she whipped her arm forward, but instead of releasing a rock, she unleashed a torrent of wind.

Hook-man's eyes widened, his mouth opening as if to yell...but then the surging gust carried him away, his scream nothing more than a sharp gasp as he was suddenly lifted and sent into the distance, his partner following him, the wooden cracks of tree branches all that remained of their presence as they became little more than pinpricks against the moonlight.

Ma shot to her feet, the burst of wind doing so just as much as the commotion that woke her. "What's going on? Ailís?! Are you alright?"

Ailís stared down at her trembling hands, her heart racing, thumping twice in quick succession just it had in her dream. Pilib rested his head in her hands to quell the tremors, to little avail. I...I...I don't know what..." she stammered. She was lifted to her feet, and when she refocused her eyes, Ma was kneeling before her, hands clasping her shoulders. It felt strange to say, "I don't know," without it being a cover to hide something she shouldn't have been doing.

It was rare that Ma seemed understanding. "Safe to say we should get out of here while you figure it out, then?" she asked.

A nod was all Ailís could manage. She picked up her bag, gesturing Pilib to crawl back inside, feeling altogether unrested.

Which only made her envious of Camaráin, who remained asleep during the entire ordeal.

Chapter Eleven

After the first hour, the war of words had grown tiresome. After the second, it had become unbearable.

How long it had been since it began, Liam could not say. All he could say for sure was that night had fallen, they were the only ones still out and about in the village, and the arguments had shifted from declarations of ineptitude to general condemnations of personal appearance and accusations of inadequacies best kept away from mixed company.

Worse still, he had been ordered by Lord Saibhir to remain where he was. For hours, Liam could do nothing but sit atop the stage long since abandoned of its intended recital and kick at workes and clods of dirt while listening to the words exchanged between Saibhir and the rotation of Inquisitors who stood before him.

If death were to have claimed him at that moment, it wouldn't have been the worst thing to happen (that spot would be claimed by some unsavory things he did up north years ago, but at least it gave him a promising new career as a ~~smuggler~~ legitimate trader). He was hungry, he was tired, bugs were biting at his mud-soaked arms and legs, he had an itch somewhere it'd be impolite to scratch while in public—it was quite a rough time for him.

Earlier, it had been easier to pass the time whilst kept here by people watching, but given the moon was high in the sky and most of the village had retired to bed—save for those who had lodged noise complaints with Inquisitors passing by, who would, in turn, attempt to pass the complaints along to their offending comrades, only to join in the festivities of this nonviolent donnybrook to create only further noise complaints—there had been no one who could otherwise entertain Liam for some time.

The only people he had seen for the better part of the last hour were the two Inquisitors standing off to the side—one of impressive height, the other of unimpressive and dirty armor. He recognized the tall Inquisitor from the recital. They were both waiting in silence, arms crossed, kicking their feet at the mud much like he had been doing, shuffling in place, and altogether looking like children waiting for their mother to finish talking to someone at the market so they could show her a cool bug they found.

Recognizing Lord Saibhir's row with the argumentative Inquisitors was going nowhere fast, Liam opted to at least humor the two standing in wait. "You two," he called. "What d'you need?"

The tall one looked over first—or at least it appeared he did. His face was obscured by a nearby awning. "Ah, yes," he said. "We were hoping to have a word with Lord Saibhir, but..."

Liam gestured at the argument. "As you can tell, Lord Saibhir is otherwise indisposed at the moment. Again, what d'you need?"

"Do you speak for him, then? Earlier today, it seemed he was ready to set us upon you."

"I speak for myself, sir, but I am not as occupied as he is, so...what can I help with?"

The second Inquisitor walked forward, rubbing away brown smears from the sigil of his cuirass. He wasn't doing a good job of—nor was he, the last hour or two he had been at it. "We had intended to request something of his lordship."

Liam rolled his eyes. "If you join your brothers now, you can start shouting it at him. Wouldn't be too far out of place at this point."

"This requires his full attention," the tall one said. "Time is of the essence."

"Is it now?" Liam asked, raising an eyebrow. "Must not be if you're standing around."

"The last request did not go so well," the dirty Inquisitor muttered, indicating to the brown marks on his armor.

"What, did you ask to enter a business accord with him? I wouldn't recommend it." Liam rose to his feet and shook his head, kicking a nearby rock. The force of it launched the rock into the knee of one of Saibhir's guards.

The tall Inquisitor shook his head. "No, we are in need of writs of investigation and questioning, and only Lord Saibhir can grant them to us."

Liam stopped before kicking a second rock at Saibhir's other guard, knocking the man to the ground with a howl of pain as he clutched his knee, his bladeless hilt falling off the sword belt. Turning his head and furrowing his brow, Liam said, "I'm sorry, writs of *what*?"

"Of investigation and questioning," the tall one repeated.

"What the devil are those?"

The Inquisitors exchanged looks with one another, the shorter and dirtier one scratching his head, while the giant could very well have been scratching his head, or he could have been fixing the awning; it wasn't quite clear.

"We...were told we needed them in order to investigate something further," admitted the ill-armored man.

Letting the silence hang between them, Liam opened his mouth, licked his lips, and asked, "By whom?"

"The...mother of that girl you accused this morning. The girl who—"

"I know what girl I accused!" Liam shouted. He closed the gap between himself and the Inquisitors, bringing himself to eye level with the shorter one and about waist-height with the taller. He wasn't going to bother straining his neck to shoot daggers into that one's eyes. "Where are they now?"

"They left," the tall man said.

"They *left*?! When?"

The quick raising of the Inquisitor's arms indicated a shrug. "Six, seven...hours ago."

"Six or seven *hours*?!"

"Maybe more. It was around midday."

Liam gritted his teeth and muttered beneath his breath, "You idiots." Before they could question him, he turned and marched toward Lord Saibhir. By now, even more Inquisitors had joined the argument—which had since shifted to disagreements of the merits of beans on toast—and villagers had begun to filter out of their homes. Liam didn't know whether to feel dismay at disturbing the peace for so long or relief at these folk seeing their Inquisitors for the rubes they were. When he drew nearer to the red-faced and hoarse-throated Saibhir, he shouted, "My lord!"

"What?!" Lord Saibhir responded, his voice an odd croak that enunciated each letter with varying volumes.

"They've escaped with the eggs."

"What? Who?!"

Liam narrowed his eyes and scrunched his nose, doing all in his power not to exclaim, "Are you daft?" There wasn't much power in those bones, and he therefore failed.

The lingering arguments—or loud roundtable discussions, as they had since become—ceased, and the Inquisitors and Saibhir all looked at Liam with incredulity. "What did you call me, boy?" the lord asked in his booming voice.

"There's no time for this," Liam answered, far too exhausted to feel threatened. "The girl and her family have been gone for hours. They have the eggs!"

Rage flared in Saibhir's eyes. "What?! Why was this not brought to my attention?"

Liam pointed his finger at the two Inquisitors trying to hide in the corner. The tall one had no chance, but at least the shorter one could hide behind his larger comrade. "These fools were under the impression they'd need 'writs of investigation and questioning' from you to seize those eggs."

"Writs of what? There's no such thing!"

"Really?" Liam questioned, widening his eyes with mock surprise. "You don't say! Perhaps this could have been settled had you not wasted the day away!"

"Do not blame the idiocy and ineptitude of the Inquisition on me, ~~smuggler~~ legitimate trader!" Saibhir frowned. "~~Smuggler~~ Legitimate trader!" He grunted with derision. "Why the devil can I not say ~~smuggler~~ legitimate trader?" He shook his head, ignoring the offended glares of the Inquisitors. "To hell with it. Guards! We set off!"

"Yes, sir!" exclaimed his guards. More so the one still in possession of the sword steel. The one Liam kicked a rock at still writhed on the ground in pain, grasping his knee. He crawled after his liege, leaving a trench of mud in his wake.

"Lord Saibhir!" Liam shouted, following after him as quickly as he could (or as quick as was necessary, in this case). "I will accompany. I will still be owed my payment once we retrieve the eggs!"

Saibhir sneered. "*Pheh*, your 'payment.' Your 'payment' is keeping your head on your shoulders, fool!"

Liam growled, clenching his hands into fists. The clink-clanking of approaching armor prevented him from doing anything rash. "And what do you idiots want?" he asked, in view of the eight Inquisitors before him.

The one directly in front, a fair-skinned man with a rich, red beard and a belly too large for his breastplate, spat on the ground before Liam's feet. "You seem to be mistaken that you will be leaving so easily."

Throwing his hand at them derisively, Liam rolled his eyes and said with a snarl, "We don't have the eggs. You've no jurisdiction over us. Now, if you'll excuse us."

"I do recall," continued the ginger-haired man, "that we intended for the High Inquisitor to sort you out. The both of you, I should say."

Liam narrowed his eyes in preparation for a rebuke, but Lord Saibhir scoffed behind him before he got the opportunity. "Why, I do believe you would need a writ of arrest for such a thing to occur. And I am under no proclivities to sign such a warrant for my own arrest, my dear men."

Spinning on his heel, mud kicking up in a tidal wave and splashing over the Inquisitors' feet, the merchant pointed an accusatory finger at the fat lord. "You *just* said there exist no such writs!"

"I believe," Saibhir responded, peering at his dirty fingernails with great interest, "such pertained to those of searching and questioning. A writ of arrest, though, seems a wondrous idea." He turned his head, neck rolls folding over the folds of his collar, and shouted, "Paper!"

One of the guards produced a damp and mud-soaked reem of paper and a quill, though from where, Liam did not want to know.

A quick scribble, punctuated with a flourish, was all Saibhir needed to seal Liam's fate. He tossed it in the direction of the Inquisitors, uncaring as to whether it reached them, and absconded into his carriage, the horse taking off before the crawling guard could board.

Liam tried to snatch the paper out of the air before it was taken, but the red-haired Inquisitor beat him to the punch. Before he knew it, he had been overpowered, the two Inquisitors locking his arms behind him, all the while he heard the gathering onlookers wondering why such writs had never been discussed at length in the first place. Without protest, he allowed the Inquisitors to drag him along to wherever they would, and as he caught a glance at the scrap of paper in the red-haired Inquisitor's hands, he could not help but fume at what was on it.

A scratch of ink that only said, "Arrest him." It may have been misspelled.

Chapter Twelve

"And here we are," Ma proclaimed as the dense woodlands loomed ahead. "The Crann Woods."

Ailís stared at the tall oaks claiming view of the northern horizon, a strange sensation caressing her arms as she drew nearer to them. "How do we know that Uncle Iósaf is in these woods?"

"Because he wrote me a letter six years ago saying, 'I'm in the Crann Woods. Here's a map if you ever want to visit.'"

"Did you bring the map?"

"It wasn't a good map, Ailís. All he did was draw a squiggly line and punctuate it with an X."

The day's long march to the Crann Woods had been marked with her growing curiosity about the mysteries within, enough to distract Ailís from the sudden power she had come into the night before. The teachings of the Priory of the Thrice-Dead Prophet spoke of the forest as a spiritual nexus where the creatures of the fae were more apt to commune with humanity.

However, whether they meant it as a threat or merely as information was up for interpretation. It was said that, "Only madmen would seek to dwell within, but you could meet a gnome, which is fun." (From *The Book of Bob*, verse 8, line 4.)

Ailís could not speak to the truth of the claim that only madmen would live in the Crann Woods, but if Uncle Iósaf was the target demographic, then who was to say?

Ailís wrapped her arm around Camaráin as they reached the forest border. Her brother had gone pale the closer they approached to the woods, but he always believed the Priory's teachings that the fae were more threatening. His white knuckles wrapped around the strap of his messenger bag were proof enough of that.

"Are you ready, kids?" Ma asked, holding her hand out to the both of them. Though the exhausted bags beneath her eyes were ever present and likely never to leave, there was an air of hope surrounding her that had not been present in some time. Her smile appeared genuine.

"Aye, aye, Ma," Ailís responded, clutching her brother ever closer. Pilib poked his head out of Ailís's bag and squawked as though to voice his own readiness.

"Cam?" Ma prompted.

A shudder rumbled through Camaráin's body, but he managed a nod. "I'm ready."

From the moment they passed into the woods, the air changed. It was dense and humid, almost oppressive, but not hot. It was more a shift in energy than anything else, like the world was alive in a way Ailís had never before experienced. The earth below was softer, the trees swaying with a breeze that should not have been present within those tight confines. Even the natural noise of the woods took on something different, the whistling of the breeze through the branches above coming off as melodic, each step taken adding a percussion to the song.

Camaráin clasped Ailís's hand and would not let go. She pulled her brother close, allowing him to feel safe in these unfamiliar environs. Even as she did, Camaráin refused to open his eyes or his mouth—the latter she would have considered a mercy in normal circumstances.

The further they drew into the Crann Woods, though, a strange rustling around them grew more apparent. Ailís expected Pilib to exhibit some protective aggression, but he was strangely the calmest out of all of them.

Though Ailís took comfort in that, it was fleeting. The rustling was soon accompanied by eyes, watchful and glowing and in varying shapes and sizes. They flitted through the shadows cast by the mighty oaks. Ailís's hands shook, one drenched in sweat as it clasped her brother's (though whose sweat it was could not be determined), and the other felt for the chilled warmth of Pilib's scales. The dragon still remained content.

Regardless, Ailís looked at her ma, her teeth chattering. "Ma...are we gonna be okay?" The double-thumping in her chest had grown intense, one thump more dominant than the other.

Ma held out her hand as though to will calmness into her daughter. "Yes, Ailís. Everything will be fine. Your uncle would not lead us astray like this."

As if on cue, the path behind them darkened, the pinprick of light signaling a return to the familiar Nóran plains obstructed by a wall of creatures flittering about. Some hovered in the air, tiny wings keeping them afloat, while others stayed low to the ground, hunched over.

A sharp scream escaped Ailís. Pilib skirted up her arm, perching atop her shoulder, but if it was a show of protection, it seemed to have been drawn more from her yelp than the presence of these creatures. Fae creatures, if the teachings of the Priory were true.

They did not draw nearer, regardless. Those watchful eyes remained affixed upon them, but no more than that.

"What do we do, Ma?" Ailís asked, her voice shaking.

Ma put a hand on Ailís shoulder, avoiding Pilib's long, scaly tail. "Just back away slowly. We'll be fine."

A muffled cry rumbled in Camaráin's mouth. The boy's eyes were clutched shut, tears falling.

Rapid footsteps filtered in on either side of them, the same eyes glowing in the darkness. Though hesitant to lock gazes with them, Ailís chanced it, watching the luminous pinpricks flittering about in the shadows, following the family's every step. A pit formed in her stomach as she looked at the rows of golden eyes floating against pitch black. That the creatures' observance of them was done in silence made it all the more unsettling, but Ailís did not feel any malice. She felt comfort in that Pilib was not tense, at least.

All paths were blocked, save the one they had been sauntering down, and to turn their backs on the creatures seemed a poor idea. Their options were limited: continue along their intended path, or they could try to go back the way they came in the hopes the creatures would disperse.

It was evident that neither choice worked, for they opted to go with a third option: stay exactly where they were and try not to soil themselves from fright. Just a family of three and their newborn dragon locked in a staring contest with creatures of the fae. It was a sound strategy. How long they spent practicing the strategy, Ailís could not say.

Against all odds, though, the plan worked. As Ailís rooted herself in place, a deep, gentle voice resounded through the woods. Whatever the voice was saying was not any tongue with which Ailís was familiar—the words came across as guttural in stark contrast to the person's soothing tone. When the words stopped, the eyes closed one by one, footsteps scattering back into the depths of the woods, until finally Ailís could no longer feel the creatures' looming presence. She breathed a sigh of relief, though such relief was fleeting. Atop her shoulder, Pilib tensed and dug his claws into her, baring his teeth. Something was approaching. Or some*one*.

"So, my map worked out well after all, did it?" The same voice echoed around them. A familiar voice that Ailís had not heard in a long time.

She turned, her heart filling with anticipation. The shadows within the forest coalesced into the form of a man, broad-shouldered and broad-bellied, long and wavy brown hair falling past his shoulders and framing a heavily-bearded face. A wide smile revealed a row of large white teeth.

Camaráin shied behind Ailís while Ma grunted at the man's approach. But Ailís could not stop smiling.

"Perfect timing," Uncle Iósaf said. "I just made stew."

Chapter Thirteen

Ailís had never liked stew. Give her a nice soup any day, and she would be happy. Heavy meat soup, though? Hard pass.

Regardless of the promise—or threat—of fresh stew, Ailís could not contain her excitement and she rushed toward her uncle and leaped into his arms, heedless of Pilib falling from her shoulder and thumping against the ground with a squawk.

Iósaf struggled to remain standing (or pretended to be weaker than he led on, which was always a possibility) and dropped to a knee, throwing his arms around Ailís. "Hey there, kiddo," he whispered. "I missed you dearly."

Ailís nuzzled against his chest, saying, "I missed you, too." When last she had seen him, she could barely wrap her arms around him. Despite the fact her arms were much longer now than when she was five years old, she still couldn't. The man may have gotten wider in the intervening years.

Her uncle pulled away and offered her his familiar smile. "You've gotten so big," he said, his voice breaking. Next, he peered over Ailís's shoulder and called, "And look at you, big man. I hardly recognized you!"

Turning, Ailís watched as Camaráin shuffled behind Ma's

legs, only hazarding a glance at Uncle Iósaf before hiding again. It was easy for Ailís to forget her brother had only been a year old when their uncle left. He hardly knew the man.

Ma cleared her throat while Iósaf's attention lingered on the boy. She had a smile on her face, though it was far less lively.

Iósaf nodded and rose to his feet, shoving his hands into his pockets. He took two steps toward Ma, but no more than that. "Hey, big sis."

A moment's silence, and Ma coolly responded, "Little brother."

After smacking his lips for a few seconds, he asked, "Did you get my letters?"

"You mean the one letter you sent six years ago? Yeah, I did, Iósaf."

"Great, great. The postmen still do a great job, then." His smile appeared forced.

Ailís turned her head one way and the next, observing the silence between her ma and uncle with great discomfort. One time, she had read a story about a family reunion where they had celebrated with one another long into the night, and many of them woke up the next morning feeling sick. Ma refused to explain the reasoning for their sudden illness, but Ailís wondered if this reunion was done to prevent falling to sickness the next day.

It was the first family reunion she had ever attended, and therefore, it was the best.

Iósaf clapped his hands. "I hope the fae folk didn't scare you too much. They're not territorial, they just don't see humans all that much."

Ma grunted. "Kind of you to learn their tongue. Seems

you've become a great neighbor, after all."

"Good folk, once you get to know 'em. Sometimes they let me help them set traps for unsuspecting wanderers. Speaking of which, how about that stew?" He rubbed his palms, an expectant smile appearing.

The question was met with silence. Camaráin's eyes went wide and he hid behind Ma.

"That was a joke," Iósaf added. "Sorry, fae humor is much more morbid."

"I pray that's the only one of your tastes to have changed since we last heard from you," Ma muttered, narrowing her eyes.

"I wouldn't say it's the only one. I eat vegetables now, too."

"That's not as impressive as you think, Iósaf. You're thirty-two years old."

"Call me a late bloomer." He stopped and cleared his throat. "Anyway, we can stand around here all we want, but I'd hazard a guess you didn't come all this way to see your exiled brother on a whim. And I take it that you've run into trouble because of that little one." He gestured to the side.

Ailís noticed he was pointing to her. "Hey! It's not my fault." She stopped and considered the claim before softly adding, "Not entirely, anyway."

"Uh, no, sorry, kiddo. Your new friend crawled behind you."

Before she could turn to look, Pilib began scurrying up her leg and perched atop her shoulder. He squawked at Iósaf and spread his wings. Ailís was unsure if Pilib was greeting him or threatening to bite his head off. One could have led to the next, but that was not yet for her to know.

Uncle Iósaf trembled, his lip twitching, though for what

reason, Ailís couldn't tell. He regained his composure after a moment, and added, "I have a million questions about that, but it would be wise not to linger here. Come along, my cottage is just up the road."

"The irresponsible brother has become a homeowner," Ma muttered. "Fancy that."

"Hey, there's a good market here. I got the place for a steal." Iósaf turned on his heel and walked back the way he came, waving his family along. "Come now, this way."

Ailís nodded to her ma and brother, and scratched Pilib under the chin to indicate he should furl his wings once more before following Iósaf. The forest path winded through the rows of tall and indistinguishable trees, and the shadows cast from above basked the road ahead in darkness. How Iósaf knew the way was beyond her, but perhaps the eyes still flickering in the wooden depths guided him.

Her apprehension faded as they emerged into a clearing, light beaming down from an undetermined source. A humble cottage came into view, a single story dwelling crafted of straw and wood, perhaps a bit too small of height for someone of Iósaf's stature. To the left of the house lay plots of flowers bearing a gorgeous pallet of colors, and opposite those was a vegetable garden from which tomatoes, carrots, and leafy greens could be seen growing.

"Ho there, Adhamh!" Iósaf shouted as they came into the clearing. "I've returned with company."

Ailís was surprised by the prospect of her uncle finding a friend in the Crann Woods, and even more so when she saw the "friend" emerge from the garden. He came up to no higher than Iósaf's knees, his face obscured by a gray, tangled mess of a beard loosely tied into two braids. A half-buttoned red shirt was rolled up to his sleeves and tucked into plain brown trousers, and wispy strands of long hair were hidden under a knit red hat. She recognized him as a gnome. One of the books back at their house in Baile went into detail about the physical characteristics of gnomes, but she didn't expect a real one to look like a tiny man.

"Adhamh," Iósaf said as he strolled to the gnome. "I'd like you to meet my family. My sister Máirín, my niece Ailís, and my nephew Camaráin." He gestured to each of them as he said their names.

Adhamh took a cursory glance at them, barked something in the fae tongue, and marched back to the garden to resume whatever he had been doing.

Iósaf bit at his lip and nodded with a raised brow.

"What did he say?" Ailís asked, eyes kept on the gnome.

Shaking his head, Uncle Iósaf said, "Nothing kind enough for your ears. We should head inside before he decides to...'greet' you some more."

It wasn't until they reached the door that Ailís realized just *how* small the house was. Iósaf had to practically crouch to fit through the door. Even Ailís nearly bumped her head on the doorframe.

Inside was much roomier, almost incomprehensibly so. A central lounge greeted them as they entered with a large wooden table placed in the middle, framed by an arrangement of chairs of equivalent make and quality, with a sofa tucked away in the corner, a wool blanket thrown atop it and hiding what looked to be a pillow. Two doors were open to the side, one revealing a large bedroom and the other exuding a smell that could only indicate the presence of a chamber pot, while opposite the doors led to a kitchen. Across the entryway lay an ornate door carved in oak with scribblings etched in the bottom.

Iósaf ushered the family to the table and motioned them to take their seats. "Welcome, welcome! I'll throw the kettle on." He retreated into the kitchen.

As the children eagerly scraped their chairs against the hardwood floor and sat, Ma looked over her shoulder, Adhamh's shadow indicating he was still hard at work in the garden. "Your...gardener? Should we invite him in, as well?"

"Oh, no," Iósaf said with a chuckle. "He's far too angry for that. He tends to only come inside once I've gone to sleep."

Ailís glanced at the sofa. "It's nice of you to let him stay here, though."

"Well, I wasn't going to completely kick him out. This house *was* his once."

Ma cleared her throat. "So, when you said you got the place for 'a steal,' do you mean...?"

A kettle clanged in the kitchen. "I won the house quite legitimately, thank you! Adhamh simply does not know when to quit while he's ahead. Terrible poker face, too."

"You won his house in a game of poker?"

"No. Tic-tac-toe."

Her mouth agape, Ma appeared dumbstruck. She shook her head in disbelief.

For her part, Ailís wondered why she hadn't won anything for all the times she beat Camaráin at tic-tac-toe. She nudged him with her elbow at the thought, but he only answered with a shrug.

"Okay, clear the way! Hot soup coming through!" Iósaf called from the kitchen. He came in with the kettle. Ailís was disappointed there was no soup.

Steam billowed out from the kettle spout as it was set upon the table with a loud thump. Pilib jumped at the noise, unfurling his wings to threaten the metal monster.

"Well, then," Iósaf said, clapping. "Now that we have you settled, I suppose I must ask..." He practically leaped over the table to the other side. Well, leaped was a strong word. It was more accurate to say he attempted to do so, but caught his foot on the edge and *flipped* over it, but at least he landed on his feet and managed not to kick either of the children. He crouched beside Ailís, eyes wide. "Just *where* did you come across your little friend here?" He glared at Pilib, the dragon matching the gaze, wings still not withdrawn.

Up close, Ailís could tell the twitching lip from earlier was not a trick of the eye. An excited tremor had gripped her uncle in a way she had never seen before. "Um...well...I found him?"

Ma crossed her arms. "Yes, *I'm* well aware you 'found' him. However, you never told me *how* you found him."

Uncle Iósaf nodded, though if he was meant to match Ma's accusatory tone, he did not get the memo. "Yes, *please* tell!"

Ailís flashed a smile. "Well...his egg fell out of a wagon."

"It 'fell?'" Ma asked.

"From a wagon, you say?" Iósaf added.

"A...merchant's wagon, yes," Ailís admitted.

"Ailís, am I correct to assume," Ma said, "that this 'merchant' is the same man who accused you of 'stealing his eggs?'"

"Well, first of all, I don't know why he said 'eggs' when I only found Pilib's egg. And second, I didn't...'steal' the egg from him because it's not like I climbed *into* his wagon or anything like that..."

"How did the dragon's egg 'fall' out of the merchant's wagon?"

Ailís maintained her nervous smile and said, "I dug a hole in its path and the wagon broke when it went over it."

Ma buried her head in her hands, loosing a loud groan. "So, you mean to say, the reason we've had a smuggler, Lord Saibhir, and the Inquisition after us is because you decided to play a prank on them?"

No denying that. Ailís quickly nodded and said, "Yep."

Ma shot her eyes toward Camaráin, who was clutching his messenger bag close to his chest. "And you helped her, I presume?"

Camaráin didn't turn around. "Uh-huh." He clutched his bag and shuffled in place.

"Oh, Heaven above..." Ma said, covering her face with her hands.

Uncle Iósaf, for his part, could only laugh and applaud. "Oh, outstanding! I'm so proud of you both!"

"Iósaf!" Ma exclaimed, incredulous.

"Oh, come off it, Máirín. You should be proud of them, too. They're smart enough not to fall for the Inquisition's lies!" He inclined his head toward her. "I presume the same of you, then."

Ma rolled her eyes and crossed her arms, looking away. "You speak as though they're engaging in an act of protest. All they did was..." She sighed and shook her head. "...'find' an egg. For good or ill, you've left your mark on them. Ailís hasn't shut up with 'Uncle Iósaf said this' and 'Uncle Iósaf said that' for the past six years."

Ailís furrowed her brow at the remark, reaching over to run her hand down Pilib's neck. She hadn't realized the dragon had yet to have furled his wings, but he finally did at her touch.

Uncle Iósaf smiled at the sight. He rose his hand pet the dragon just the same but withdrew when Pilib bared his teeth. "Well, I'd wager you'd agree that by this point the dragon isn't capable of great evil or little evil or any sort of evil, yes?"

"If he takes after Ailís, who's to say?" Ma flashed a glance at her daughter, though it was clear that she was only teasing.

"Heh," Iósaf chuckled. "If he was a hellspawn, I'm sure half the country would have been razed by now." He walked around the perimeter of the table, tussling Camaráin's hair on the way by, and made his way toward the large ornate door. "Only confirms what anyone with a brain has been saying for generations."

"Oh? And what's that?"

With a grin, Iósaf kicked at the door. His foot connected with a loud thud. The door did not open, and he groaned in pain.

"Are you okay?" Ailís cried, shooting up to her feet.

Hissing in a pained breath, Iósaf raised a hand to indicate he was fine. "There didn't used to be a doorknob here." From the ground, he reached up and turned the doorknob and pushed the door open until it thumped to a stop on the other side. His foot clearly still tender, he hopped to a standing position and extended his arms at his side.

Whatever grandeur and theatrics he was trying to convey were lost, but Ailís's eyes still widened in wonder at what waited behind him: a vast library, the walls lined with tomes big and small.

"Generations upon generations of disenfranchised draconic scholars can't be wrong." He put weight on his foot. "Ow."

Chapter Fourteen

Ailís approached the library with her mouth open, disbelieving the sight. The walls were lined with bookshelves, and not a space was vacant. She had never seen so many books in one place, let alone tomes on the subject of dragons (beyond the Inquisition-sanctioned early reader selection from the *Dragons and You: Don't You Do It!* series that she often found at school).

It was all she could do not to drool.

That was not lost on Uncle Iósaf. Whatever pain that had gripped his foot had been fleeting enough for him to file in beside her to share in her mirth. He smiled at her, but one look in his eyes was all that was needed to confirm that he was smiling through the pain.

"Beautiful, isn't it?" he said, resting his hand against the doorframe. "Hundreds of years of knowledge and scholarship passed through generations of the order of Draconic Priests. A treasure trove greater than any bounty."

Ailís craned an eyebrow. "Draconic Priests? I've never heard of them."

Iósaf grunted. "Few have. I'd be surprised if any still exist, thanks to the Inquisition." He frowned, shaking his head.

"Long ago, before the Inquisition, they were the heralds and missionaries of the dragons of Nóra. The Inquisition changed all that, and now, their legacy remains only in the tomes they left behind." He walked—trying his hardest to hide his limp and failing miserably—toward one of the stacks of books on the floor and picked up the top tome. On the spine could be read, *A Short History of Long Days: The Early Years of the Inquisition*.

"I suppose it was no small task to have amassed such a collection," Ma said, wandering over to the library, her hand resting on Camaráin's shoulder as she dragged him along.

"Oh, no, it was," Iósaf responded. "These books were Adhamh's to begin with. Why do you think I played him for the house?"

"It's a wonder he's not bludgeoned you in your sleep."

"Gnomes aren't violent, they're just angry. At this point, his grumbling lulls me to sleep."

"Oh, sweet mercy," Ma mumbled.

Ailís stepped into the library and stood in awe of the collection. There was even a shelf above the door marked with the label, "Actual Propaganda." She squinted at the spines, the lettering hard to make out, but recognized one book. "Hey, Cam! It's that book you were reading the other day?"

Her brother's ears perked up. "Which one?" he asked, walking into the library, still clutching the strap of his bag.

"*Gnomes, Faeries, Selkies, and Other Fae Creatures Approved by High Inquisitor Dónal That Aren't Evil Dragons.*"

"Oh, right. That book was terrible. It didn't even talk about any fae creatures. It just listed the creatures and put a check mark next to them."

"That's about the size of those books penned by the Inquisition," Iósaf said, looking up from the tome he was holding. "Nothing more than fear-mongering for those who don't know any better."

"Why do you have them, Uncle Iósaf?" Ailís wondered.

"Now those, I *did* collect. Figure the fewer of them out there, the better. Guess you could say I'm doing a service for the people of Nóra. If I have to see one more false account of the Inquisitors' 'holy quest,' I think I'm going to puke."

Ailís glanced at the book her uncle was holding. "Does *that* book make you puke?"

Her uncle chuckled and looked at the cover of the book again, seeming to have not realized what book he had taken, only to flip through the pages on reflex. "No, kiddo, this one just makes me sad."

"Sad?"

He nodded. "Sad that the Inquisition started because of something as stupid as fear."

"What did they have to be afraid of?" As if on cue, Pilib slithered along the ground and scurried onto Ailís's shoulder. She scratched under his chin. "When Pilib hatched, being afraid was the last thing on my mind."

"Then, you're smarter than most." Iósaf snapped the book shut. "I'm sure you've been bored to death by the Inquisition's accounts of its origins and how they discovered the dragons were capable of tremendous evil and needed to be purged from our land. How they pushed them out of Nóra and beyond the Cliffs of Ard—which never made sense to me as being a 'purge' when it was in truth a diaspora, but perhaps that's a concept too advanced for the folks of Nóra to understand. Ah, well, I digress.

"But whatever you want to call it—a purge, a banishment, a scaly heave-ho—it started due to fear. The fear of the connection between a dragon and the one with whom they bond upon hatching. Seeing as how Pilib never leaves your side, it's easy to assume that you've achieved a bond with him."

Ailís nodded. "Yeah, we bonded right from the start! I threw him a birthday party after he hatched, and—"

Iósaf held up a hand. "That's not what I mean. Before the Inquisition, there would be a spiritual connection between a dragon and their chosen human. Think of it as a tether, forever linking them. Not only would their bonded share in their emotions, but they would be bestowed a sliver of power over the elements. Air, water, earth, fire—each dragon was born with an affinity toward one of them, and should they bond with a human, that person would be able to summon the strength of the elements at will."

"That...I...I see." Ailís stared down at her hands, the cool sensation of dense air still lingering on her fingertips. "I may have done that already. There were a couple of thieves who tried to take Pilib from me the other night, and I..."

"So, that's what happened," Ma muttered.

Taking a seat, Iósaf crossed his legs—hissing back another pang of pain in his foot—and nodded. "And anything else? Strange dreams, voices, unfamiliar sensations?"

Ailís furrowed her brow. "All of that, I think. I have dreams where I'm flying like a dragon. The other night, a voice I didn't know was telling me to wake. Even my heartbeat feels...weird."

"No need to be worried, kiddo." Iósaf's smile was warm. "You're just in sync with what Pilib's feeling. You've bonded with a dragon! Probably the first to do so since before the

Inquisition! We ought to celebrate!"

"Iósaf," Ma said, a warning in her voice. "Shouldn't we be concerned that Ailís is coming into something a bit...unnatural?"

He was quick to that aide. "Ah, dear sister, that's just generations of fear and misinformation rotting your brain."

"Iósaf!"

Ailís giggled, failing to stifle it behind her hand. She had to look away when Ma began to stare daggers at her, her eyes scanning the tomes covering a wide range of topics, from draconic biographies to travel guides to a book titled, *How to Commit Tax Evasion in Three Gnomish Steps*. That one may have been misplaced.

"The only thing that's unnatural," Iósaf continued, "is pretending a natural part of our people and history to be something worthy of shame."

"What do you mean?" Ma asked.

Rising back to his feet, Iósaf limped over to a book called *Interview With the Dragonfire*. He flipped it open, coughed, and tossed it back on the shelf. "Apologies, that's for my, um...alone time reading. What I really wanted was...ah, here we are." He picked up another book, the words on the spine illegible to Ailís's eye. "Generations ago, we lived in harmony with the dragons. We paid them ample respect and adulation, and in return, they would bestow upon us their blessings: bountiful harvests, fair weather, wealth of heart, good health. It was a beautiful balance between despite of the world of differences separating us. At least until the First Inquisitor Peadar guffed that up for everyone and decided that our relationship with dragons was unnatural."

"'And so the First Inquisitor led the righteous and true defenders of the Thrice-Dead Prophet to slay and/or hand eviction notices to the wicked dragons,'" Ma said, finishing the oft-recited tale of the Inquisition's humble beginnings.

Iósaf scoffed. "If only that held even an iota of the truth. 'First Inquisitor' Peadar was eaten within five minutes. His close chums got real cross about that and started chanting his name in the streets like he was a martyr."

Ailís inclined her head. "But the First Inquisitor was made a Saint by the Priory! We learned that in school. That means everything about the Inquisition was a lie!"

"Most good stories begin with a lie, kiddo," her uncle said with a nod. He looked at his shelves—not Adhamh's shelves, *his* shelves—and added, "Well, not these stories. These are all true, and they're all good. Some are helpful, too, for the day-to-day. I had a book in here on taxes. Where did I put it...?"

"All that aside," Ma said, raising a hand, "it should have been easy for the dragons to defend themselves, no? If the First Inquisitor was not a great tactician like he's raised up to be, then..."

"Think for a moment: if you were marked as a being of pure evil, would you then act in a way that only affirms as much?" Iósaf extended his hands in a placating gesture. "The dragons of Nóra, by their very nature, are nonviolent. They wanted nothing more than to live in harmony with us, but their peaceful nature made it easier for the Inquisition to drive them away beyond the Cliffs of Ard, where reaching them is nigh-impossible, save for those with enough dedication, curiosity, or gambling arrears to motivate them. And thus, the Draconic Highlands were established not as a place of exile and shame, but as a bastion where they were removed from the ignorance of man. A shame they took all the blessings of good weather with them, though. Would be nice to have more than a day or two of sunshine a year." He closed the book, placing it back cover-down on the edge of shelf, likely to read later.

Ma walked over to Ailís, her brow furrowing as she glanced at her daughter. "But what role does she play in this?"

"What 'role?'" Iósaf asked. He shrugged. "Does she need a role? We're not characters in some grand epic to rise against the corrupt and wicked. She's not a chosen hero. She's just the right person for the right dragon." He winked at Ailís, and then set his eyes on Pilib, regarding the dragon in silence. A long, long silence. A bit too long.

"*Ahem.* Um, Iósaf?" Ma prodded.

Breaking from his trance, Iósaf shook his head and smiled again. "Right, apologies. Anyway, why don't you stay here? There's plenty of space."

Ailís's eyes widened. She turned to her ma, jumping up and down. "Can we, Ma? Please, please, please?"

Pilib flapped his wings in rhythm with Ailís's words. His squawking lacked the same rhythm.

"Now, hold on, Ailís," Ma said, raising her palm in a demand for silence. She frowned at Uncle Iósaf. "What about these...'powers' of hers? Shouldn't we be worried?"

"Bah," Iósaf muttered, limping his way back to his chair before lounging with his fingers linked behind his head. "That's a problem for tomorrow. I'm sure you want to rest."

"What about Adhamh? Will he mind? It doesn't seem like there's enough space for the three of us, plus the dragon."

"Oh, we have a whole cellar as well, provided he hasn't

changed the locks again. One time, he did it with me in there. Ho-ho, now that's a story. It was about three months ago when—"

"Another time, Iósaf." Ma's tone indicated that she did not, in fact, wish to hear this tale another time. "What about the Inquisition? Sooner or later, they'll find us. The dragon won't remain small forever."

Iósaf waved his hand in dismissal. "Oh, they never come here. Something about High Inquisitor Dónal hating the humidity or some such. His flock follows his lead without questioning, so..." He shrugged. "It's worked out for all of us here. We don't get bothered."

"'We?'" Ma repeated. "You mean it's not just you and the gnome here?"

"Huh? Oh, yeah, I should have said that earlier." A sheepish grin stretched Iósaf's lips. "We practically have a village here. We're not a hodgepodge of hermits and exiles. Well, *I* am, but that's beside the point. Most of us just like the peace and quiet. More time to read, so far as I'm concerned."

Ma stared at her brother in disbelief, though given everything, Ailís was surprised there was still anything Uncle Iósaf could do that would shock her.

Pointing toward the door, Iósaf added, "Why don't you go visit Áine down the way? Head out the house, take a left, about six or seven trees down you'll see her house. You can't miss it—it's nicer than mine and it smells wonderful."

Ma held open her hands, waiting for him to continue. "What are we meant to do at this 'Áine's' house?"

"Get some pie or something. Her baked goods are *the* best thing you will ever eat. Normally, I send Adhamh, but she'll probably appreciate someone less angry. Even if it *is* you, Máirín." He grinned.

Ailís smiled with glee. "We can get a real birthday pie for Pilib! We can throw him an actual party!" She scratched Pilib's chin. The mention of pie perked him right up. He leaped from Ailís's shoulders and scurried to the doorway before stopping to stare at her as though wondering what the holdup was.

Ma sighed and shook her head. There wasn't a way out of this. "Should you come with us?" she asked Iósaf. "Probably better that someone she knows is with us, rather than us showing up at her door demanding a pie."

Iósaf's face went white as a sheet. "Uh...no. I am...very busy right now." He reached for the nearest book and pretended to read it. The act didn't fool anyone; the book was upside down, and even then, the unbound pages slipped out from the spine. "You can make do on your own, right?"

Rolling her eyes, Ma took hold of Ailís's shoulder and made for the door. As they reached the library door, the sound of Camaráin's footsteps followed them. Ma looked over her shoulder and said, "Why don't you keep your uncle company, Cam? Have some boy time."

A hesitant frown stretched on Camaráin's face, but eventually, he nodded.

Ailís ran outside, hearing Adhamh's angry grumbling from the vegetable garden but thought it best to leave him be. On her shoulder, Pilib began to squawk in mimicry of the gnome.

When Ma emerged from the house, hand on her lower back as she straightened, she rolled her eyes and began to chart their path. "Some things never change," she muttered.

"Why didn't Uncle Iósaf want to come with us?" Ailís asked.

Ma scoffed. "Didn't you hear? He's too busy."

"He looked like he was faking it."

With a terse smile, Ma said, "You'll understand when you start talking to boys."

Chapter Fifteen

Liam opened his eyes and was surprised to be covered in even more mud. It didn't make sense—they had "cleansed" him after throwing him in this cell. They also gave him new clothes. It apparently rained mud inside this cell.

He had never seen the inside of an Inquisition jail, nor had he seen the outside of one. For all the technicalities one could employ to skirt around an Inquisitor's jurisdiction, he was surprised these cells were warranted by regional governors. Hell, he barely remembered the path taken to bring him here; he had blacked out and the next he knew, he was there.

No guards were near, nor any prisoners. He rose to his feet, surveying the filthy interior and the leaking ceiling through the bars of his cell. Dim natural light beamed into the corridor from the left, and if not for that, he would have presumed this cell to have been thrown in a hole in the ground. It was shocking how empty the place was, though. He put his hands on his hips and shook his head. "I must be the dumbest man alive to have actually been taken by the Inquisition."

Someone burped around the corner. "Not the dumbest, I reckon. Most lack that type of self-awareness." Metallic footsteps echoed in the corridor, a large frame coming into view.

The man wore the standard armor of the Inquisition, complete with its sigil bastardizing that of the Priory on whose coattails they rode, but flowing behind him was a long, red cloak, and tucked beneath a gauntleted arm was a helmet with a red plumage wafting from the top. In contrast to the armor's regal appearance was a disheveled and plump bearded face framed by dark locks of greasy hair.

Liam couldn't help but feel shocked. "High Inquisitor Dónal? How did you get here so quickly?"

The High Inquisitor puffed out his chin and looked down upon the captured merchant with an air of disdain. Dónal was the only Inquisitor who commanded the type of authority to be qualified for such an expression, and yet it still looked out of place on him. "I appear wherever I am needed, whenever I am needed. I am in all places at once, for my gaze over this beautiful land of Nóra is all-seeing and all-knowing." He burped again, and his breath was pungent.

Wincing from the stench, Liam waved away the tuft of air and said, "Probably more accurate to say you happened to be at the pub here and then passed out in one of the cells, isn't it?" He turned out his hands with a shrug. "Unless you were standing around the corner this whole time, waiting for me to speak."

Dónal pointed at Liam, inclining his head. "You're half-right and entirely correct on all accounts." He was slurring his words.

"...What?"

"Hey, *I'm* asking the questions here." Dónal cracked his knuckles, an impressive feat, given he was wearing gauntlets. "Perhaps it was providence that I found myself here today. Capital crimes *do* require my immediate attention, and I am ever eager to learn of how you came to commit one of the gravest of offenses under the laws of the Priory: possession of not only draconic paraphernalia, but the *eggs* of dragons themselves."

Liam furrowed his brow, listening to the nearby drip-drip-drip of what he hoped was water. "The Priory doesn't establish laws," he said instead. "They just don't pay taxes."

"But under the laws established by the *Inquisition* of the Priory of—"

"Yeah, yeah, yeah," Liam interrupted, brushing that aside. "Went over this with your lackeys already. By the *very letter* of the Inquisition's 'laws,' I have committed no crimes. *I* am no longer in possession of the eggs, and by keeping me here without regard for your laws, you are making a farce of your already farcical organization. Can I go home, now?"

Dónal shook his head, a deep frown on his face. "This is no simple matter, ~~smuggler~~ legitimate trader. I—wait, what did I just say?"

"You said 'legitimate trader.'"

"But I wanted to say ~~smuggler~~ legitimate trader—blast it, I did it again!"

"Don't think too hard. It's just a bit. You were saying?"

Something thumped overhead, knocking loose puffs of dust and dark droplets of water. Dónal huffed and crossed his arms, a powerful sneer on his face. "Hmph, as I was saying before I was...distracted by whatever foulness surrounds you...I cannot ignore an uproar about the presence of dragons. As the High Inquisitor, it is my duty to ensure dragons are vanquished, root and stem."

"'Root and stem?'" Liam repeated. "I believe you're confused with dragon*fruit.*"

"Wrong again! We vanquished those two hundred years ago!"

"You vanquished...some fruit."

"It's an invasive food group! It would have disrupted our ecosystem!"

Liam shrugged. "Suppose I can't argue with that." He enjoyed the fruit. Hard to acquire, though. He wouldn't mind a little ecological disruption for a bite of one.

"Therefore," Dónal shouted, his voice resounding off the bars separating them, "you must tell me *where* these dragon eggs have gone. The sanctity of Nóra depends upon it!"

"Why don't you track down Lord Saibhir?" Liam could not hide his distaste at saying the man's name.

"It was to my understanding—and to those in the village who heard you to begin with—that a little girl had the eggs in her possession, and not Lord Saibhir."

"Well, if you hurry, you may catch him. He'll have probably found them by the time you make it."

"Answer the question, ~~smuggler~~ legitimate trader—damn it, it happened again! How are you—"

"Trust me, High Inquisitor. If I had such a power, I wouldn't waste it on how you say my profession." Liam looked upward, unsure of how it happened, himself.

Dónal extended his fingers as though ready to strangle the merchant but settled for an exasperated sigh. "Just answer the question."

"I don't know what you want me to say, High Inquisitor. By the letter of the law, neither myself nor Lord Saibhir are presently committing any crimes. Therefore, you have no jurisdiction to keep me locked in here."

The High Inquisitor fished through his pockets (the presence of pockets on their armor being a common source of joy for the members of the Inquisition) and pulled out a crumpled slip of paper. "And this writ of arrest? Does this not confine you to these quarters?"

"Oh, come on, Dónal. We both know Lord Saibhir made that up today."

A blank expression was Dónal's response. "He...did?"

"Oh, for the love of..." Liam buried his face in his hands and groaned. "Yes! Why do you all not understand that there is no such thing as a writ of arrest or of investigation or questioning? Gah!" He threw his hands in the air and paced around the perimeter of his cell.

"...Oh." The High Inquisitor looked embarrassed and bewildered. "Well, don't I feel foolish."

"You should! Heaven help me, why are we relying on *you* to 'protect' our land?"

A long, awkward silence filled the valley between them. "Well..." the High Inquisitor began, his voice meager in contrast to his large frame. The discovery of his own stupidity seemed to have sobered him; he wasn't slurring his words anymore. "As pertains the contents of your wagon—I presume that is the one that has been left unattended at Lord Saibhir's estate?"

Liam threw his hands in the air again. "Probably."

"There were other...illicit goods present within. May I—"

"Were they draconic in nature?"

"I...uh, well, no."

"Then your jurisdiction begins and ends there. Release me.

By the letter of your laws, I am committing no crimes."

Dónal held up the writ of arrest again. "But what about—"

"Lord above, it's not real, Dónal! Did you even look at it?" Liam pointed at the paper. "All it says is, 'Arest him!' He didn't even spell 'arrest' correctly! It could be intended for anyone! Also, there's no such thing as a writ of arrest!"

"Fine, fine. Out you go." He reached and opened the cell without need for a key.

Immediately, Liam glanced toward the open cell. "You mean that wasn't locked to begin with?"

"Oh, we don't even have keys. You're the first person thrown in a cell in about twenty years. We melted down the locks to make our armor. It's a funny story, that. See—"

"Ugh, I don't care." Liam shoved the High Inquisitor out of his way, such that he could when faced with a man in full armor. All he could actually do was *thump* against the metal and wait for the man to move. "How do I get out?"

With a hesitant—and perhaps apologetic—smile, Dónal pointed at a set of stairs with his thumb. "Just take those stairs. We're just in the pub's cellar."

"What, how? I don't remember that happening."

"Yeah, strange things happen when you black out, huh? I've been there more time than I can count."

Liam shook his head. "I can't believe you're the High In-quisitor." He mumbled and ascended the stairs, Dónal swaying behind him. When he opened the door at the top, he groaned with disbelief. Three rows of wooden tables were filled with locals singing a song off-key, clinking tall mugs together and letting their contents overflow onto the floor. Sure enough, Liam had indeed been in the pub's cellar the whole time.

Not wanting to spend a second longer here, he rushed to exit, pushing the door open, greeted once more by the familiar stench of the crisp Baile air. His boots sank into something soft the moment he stepped outside, and he hoped it was only mud.

"So, where will you go?" the High Inquisitor asked, following him out of the pub.

Sneering, Liam said, "Away from here. What's it to you?"

Dónal held out his hands. "I have a duty to root out any evil plaguing Nóra. Meanwhile, I assume *you* might have some words for Lord Saibhir. Perhaps...our goals align, ~~smuggler~~ legitimate trader—crap, I forgot about that."

Sighing, Liam shrugged and turned toward the open fields beyond the village limits. "I saw him going north. So, we'll head there."

"Wonderful. Let's be away."

"Whatever."

As the unlikely pair made their way through Baile, Liam glanced at a crowd chanting and wielding picket signs, demanding writs of arrest and investigation be penned into law.

He couldn't wait to be done with this village.

Chapter Sixteen

The eyes of curious fae watchers were no less unsettling the second time around. It was a tall order to get used to a swarm of faeries fluttering into the clearing like inebriated butterflies.

Despite their unease, Ailís and Ma found the neighboring cottage about six or seven trees down—Iósaf wasn't being glib about it after all. For such close proximity, it felt as though there was enough separation for it to be another world unto itself.

A beautiful array of flowers lined the front of the house, painting the yard in a vibrant pastel of purples and yellows and reds. White sidings lined the cottage, a plume of smoke billowing from an opening in the straw-thatched roof. Where Iósaf's cottage was designed for the sensibilities of a gnome, this house obviously was built for a human. If anything, this was the image Ailís carried in her mind of a house in an enchanted forest: sunbeams casting a stunning light on the scene, a delicious aroma dancing on the arms of the wind, birdsong offering a beautiful melody.

Almost on cue, as she and Ma set foot in the clearing, a soft voice called out to them. "Can I help you?"

Ailís looked to her left and spotted a woman kneeling at the side of the house with a watering can, paying her new arrivals little attention as she tended to her garden. Unsure of what to say, Ailís stepped closer to her ma and wrapped a hand around the crook of her arm. She could feel Pilib rustling within her bag, his front legs desperately trying to claw their way to the opening. A nudge with her knee quelled him.

Ma cleared her throat. "Would you happen to be Áine?" she asked.

The woman turned her head, eyeing the two with suspicion. She appeared to be the same age as Uncle Iósaf, perhaps a few years younger, judging from the absence of wrinkles around her eyes. Her dark hair was tied back in a messy bun, fine strands of it dancing with the wind in front of her striking blue eyes. She walked over, brushing dirt off her freckled forearms while paying little heed to the specks marring the otherwise pristine stitching of her sweater. "Who's asking?"

"We're...I guess you could say, visiting some family in the woods. We were instructed to come and pick up some baked goods from you?"

Áine raised a curious eyebrow. "No one 'visits family' in the Crann Woods. Most have left their families."

Ma shrugged. "Would you believe me if I told you my brother is just odd?"

After a brief hesitation, Áine returned the shrug. "I suppose most of us here are."

The wonderful aroma wafted by Ailís's nose again. She couldn't help but tilt her head back and breathe deep. "And it smells like you're baking something already, so..." Despite the elbow from Ma, she still smiled.

"I'm sorry for my daughter," Ma said. "She sometimes lacks

tact."

"No, it's quite alright," Áine said, waving the concern aside with her hand. "The visitors I do receive are typically drawn by baked goods, anyway. There just haven't been many new faces around lately." She turned toward the door and waved her hand forward. "Come on, let's head inside."

Ailís pumped her fist in a show of victory, voicing the same excitement before feeling a firm and quieting hand placed over her mouth. She tilted her head away from the hand's clutches and skipped ahead, ignoring the discomfort of Pilib's hidden body thumping against her thigh. Soft grunts and squawks could be heard inside her bag as though in protest.

Enthrallment wouldn't be the word to describe the inside of Áine's home. Upon first sight, Ailís's eyes went wide. The place was cozy. The walls were lined with houseplants. Beside each window sat a large velvet chair, and beside each one was an end table upon which rested a book or a half-finished cup of tea. Shelves were mounted on the far side of the wall and sported a wide array of knick-knacks and trinkets ranging from interesting cups to little wooden figurines to cuts of intricately patterned fabrics, and beneath those sat a chest housing a variety of different yarns and knitting needles.

Ailís murmured, "Wow." She had forgotten about the promise of baked goods and started to make for the eclectic collection of trinkets. A firm hand pulled her back by the shoulder.

"Ailís!" Ma hissed. "This isn't your house. You can't just wander around."

Again, Áine waved a hand. "That's alright. I *do* have a habit of holding on to some of the little knick-knacks I find lying about.

It's always been something of a hobby of mine, ever since I was little. I lost a lot of them years ago, but being here affords me nothing but time to build the collection back up again."

The idea of there being even more of these little oddities was something Ailís wanted to know more about, but something else immediately grabbed her attention.

"Now, then," Áine said. "You were looking for some baked goods? There'll be a blackberry pie ready shortly."

Ailís jumped and spun on her heel, flashing her mismatched teeth in a wide grin. "Yes, yes!" she exclaimed. Were it not for Pilib's weight at her hip, she'd have skipped right to the kitchen.

"Well, far be it for me to keep you from it." Áine smiled and turned to Ma. "I'm sorry, I didn't catch your name."

"Oh!" Ma gasped, putting her hand to her chest. "Apologies, that was rude of me. My name is Máirín. I think you're already familiar with my daughter, Ailís."

"Very nice to meet you both," Áine said. "Well, as I said, if you'll wait a little while longer, I'll have that pie ready for—Heaven above, what is going on in there?" Her eyes shot toward Ailís, or more specifically, the rustling within her bag.

Pilib peeked his head out of the bag and squawked.

Eyes widened, Áine stared at both Ailís and Ma. "Is that..."

Ma appeared defeated. "We'll...take that pie, whenever it's ready."

"No, no, it's..." Áine sighed. "Sorry, I didn't expect to see a dragon when I awoke this morning."

Ailís froze, unsure if she had fallen into a trap. Pilib, for his part, remained visible, his mouth open in an approximation of a smile.

As for Áine, she reacted with none of the surprise that

Ailís would have expected. Instead, she appeared...somber. No greed, no anger, no wild proclamations of evil having returned to the earth. The woman merely...smiled. One filled with visible melancholy, but a smile, nonetheless. She turned her back to Ailís and Ma, and walked toward the kitchen, remaining silent.

As the minutes stretched on, and Ailís filed in beside her ma, nervous enough for the both of them, Áine at last broke the silence and called, "Who did you say suggested you come by?"

Ma cleared her throat, flashing a concerned glance at Ailís, and said, "My brother. Iósaf?"

Another silence until Áine replied, "Who?"

"Uh, he lives just up the way, about six or seven trees down? Says he usually sends a gnome named Adhamh to pick up pies."

Áine reappeared from around the corner, her brow furrowed. Her fingers were coated with flour and purple smears of liquified blackberries. "I didn't realize that gnome lived with anyone. I thought he was just some vagrant who really liked pies."

Ma turned her head and muttered, "Well, you're probably half right."

"You know, I didn't think he'd want to live with anyone. He's always struck me as too angry for that. In fact, he's angrier every time he comes."

"How often is he here?"

Áine shrugged. "Once a week? Sometimes more?"

Ailís tugged at her ma's trousers and leaned in close. "Do you think Uncle Iósaf shares any of the pies with Adhamh?" she whispered.

Ma closed her eyes, letting loose a long and deep sigh. Her

silence toward that question seemed to answer enough. "Look, why don't you come back to my brother's? It's got to be better than just...baking pies by yourself and waiting for a gnome to grab them."

A chuckle escaped Áine's lips. "I don't mind it. I moved to the Crann Woods to avoid people, not meet them. The occasional passersby are more than enough for me."

Her mind racing back to her uncle, Ailís reached into her bag and pulled Pilib out for the woman to see in full. "Please? Pilib just hatched a few days ago and I want to throw him a birthday party. He'll have fun with more people!"

"A birthday party? 'Pilib?'" Áine inclined her head toward the dragon. "You named him Pilib?"

Ailís nodded. "Uh-huh! And I think my uncle wants to meet you, too! I mean, *really* wants to meet you." She raised her eyebrows in that kind of gesture that meant, "You know what I mean."

The woman sighed, rolled her eyes, and shook her head. "Being away from leering men was another reason I moved here," she murmured.

"Preach it, sister," Ma said.

Áine scoffed, but a smile still managed to skirt across her lips. "I suppose it *would* be nice to throw a party for someone other than fae folk." Closing her eyes, she flashed her teeth at Ailís--and, more notably, at Pilib—and conceded. "Fine, then. Let's...throw a birthday party for a dragon?"

Pilib spread his wings in what seemed to be triumph.

Chapter Seventeen

Pilib flew ahead as they returned to Iósaf's cottage. Or, rather, he jumped from Ailís's shoulder and glided about five yards before crashing to the ground. A proud moment for Ailís, regardless.

As she scooped the hatchling into her arms, hushing his disgruntled squawks, Ailís noticed Adhamh stomping into the clearing, throwing his arms in the air and grumbling. The words sounded harsh, but then again, so did the fae tongue.

"Adhamh?" Ailís called, drawing the gnome's attention. "Is something the matter?"

Teeth flashing from beneath his bushy beard, Adhamh glared at her with his beady eyes and began shouting at her, his arms waving every which way as his tirade dragged on.

Whether Ailís should have been intimidated or not, she could not tell, but she was relieved he vanished behind the tall stalks of vegetables in the garden. "I think those may have been more unkind words," she said, turning to Ma and Áine.

Scoffing, Áine shrugged and replied, "That's putting it mildly."

"What did he say?" Ma asked, her curiosity seeming to be piqued.

Áine's eyes widened and she blew out a puff of breath before leaning whispering something to Ma.

"Oh, my word!" Ma exclaimed. "To shreds, you say? How would that work?"

"Believe me, that's tame compared to other things I've heard them say."

Ailís furrowed her brow and put her hands on her hips. "Hey, I want to know what he said, too!"

"No," Ma and Áine said. They pressed forward before Ailís could press the issue.

When they opened the front door—and crawled through the front door—they were greeted with the sound of an on-going conversation. Ailís smiled, gladdened by the idea of Camaráin at least working up the courage to entertain their uncle with a conversation, whatever it may have been.

"...but, there's no way to know *when* it will happen," Iósaf said. It seemed the two were still in the library. "And what causes it is hard to say."

"You haven't read anything about it?" Camaráin asked. He sounded...worried? Disappointed?

"Haven't thought to look for it. But be patient. It'll happen when it happens."

"We're back!" Ma called, bumping her head on the low doorframe. She hissed a word Ailís had once been told never to repeat, which always seemed unfair with the regularity Ma had used it.

"Oh!" Iósaf responded, the rushed sound of pages rustling and sliding along the floor accompanying his movements. "Didn't even hear you come in." Hard to believe, given how loudly the door had creaked. "Everything go well?"

"We saw Adhamh out front," Ailís said. "He seemed upset. Well, more than he was earlier."

"Ah, he probably bumped into some brigands. They always seem to catch him when he's taking a leak."

Glancing at the door to the room with the chamber pot—now closed and with a more potent smell lingering than before—Ailís asked, "Does he not...*go* inside?"

"Oh, he got mad one time when I asked him if he ever used fae magicks to disappear his leavings. Once read that in a weird book. He said that was the dumbest thing he ever heard and called me...many colorful things."

"What does that have to do with...?"

"Um, nothing. I would just...watch your step, is all."

It was not lost on Ailís the look of revulsion on Áine's face. The woman sneered in the direction of the library, narrowing her eyes.

Ma, as she was wont to do, buried her face in her hands and mouthed, "I'm sorry."

"Anyway!" Iósaf exclaimed as the rustling ceased. "Judging from the smell, I'd say you've brought back something delicious. So, how about we—" He stepped into the main foyer, Camaráin closed behind him, and his mouth dropped. He froze in place, his eyes locked on Áine, the woman maintaining her disapproving stare, and . . .

Whatever came out of his mouth was not of the Nóran tongue, if they were words at all. Iósaf's face grew red, rivulets of sweat streaming down his face. His hands shook and he ran them through his tangled mass of hair, the mystery words still billowing from his mouth, until finally—and perhaps mercifully—he nudged Camaráin out of the way and gestured to Áine in what appeared to be a salute and shut the library door.

A muffled noise erupted from the other side of the door. The words were indiscernible, but there was a repetition of, "Stupid! Stupid!" that was clear enough for all to hear.

After an uncomfortably quiet minute, Áine harumphed and placed the blackberry pie on the table. "Right," she said. "It was lovely to meet you both, but I think now would be a good time for me to—"

"No, please!" Ailís exclaimed. "My uncle loves your pies and wanted to meet you! He probably just didn't say the fae words right!"

"He wasn't speaking the fae language," Áine asserted, raising an eyebrow.

"...Oh."

To the side, Ma shook her head with bemusement. "Always was the smooth talker with women, that one."

As Iósaf's anguished cries continued from within the library, Ailís grasped Áine's hands. "Please, Áine? You did promise to help us throw a birthday party for Pilib."

"We're throwing a party?" Camaráin asked, running up to the table. Whatever disappointment that had colored his words earlier was now gone and replaced with excitement. He sniffed the pie, and his eyes lit up. "I don't know who you are, lady, but please stay!" Not even Ma's admonishing words could diminish the revelry waiting to burst from him.

Even Pilib got in on the act, leaping from Ailís's shoulder and landing atop the backrest of the chair nearest to Áine—or rather, crashing into the back of the chair and cracking the wood, but he still scampered up to perch atop it. He stared at Áine, widening his eyes in a way Ailís had only ever seen puppies do, and let loose a low squawk that resembled a whimper.

Áine stared at the dragon, her lower lip quivering. Gritting her teeth, she let her bag drop off her shoulder and into her hand and started to empty its contents onto the table. "Fine, fine. You win."

The children—and Pilib—cheered, while Iósaf continued to wail.

Chapter Eighteen

"That's the last time I letcha bring me to the Crann Woods," Ciarán said, scratching at the nub of his arm where his hook used to be.

"Come off it, Ciarán," Tomás said, rolling his eyes. "You've been sayin' that fer years."

"Aye, and every time we come here, a gnome starts attackin' us while he's mid-stream! Don't know why ya keep tryin' it."

"D'you want a new hook for yer hand or no? Fae folk got some of the best iron for it."

"Don't think they've got the best of anythin' 'side from the angriest gnomes."

"Don't know 'bout that. Y'ever been to the capital? Those late-night breakfast places have *the* angriest gnomes for their wait staff. Grand slam ya in the face, they will, if you're cross with'em."

Ciarán grumbled. It had been a long day. A long, painful day. He was always happy to see the light at the end of the Crann Woods. The place gave him the creeps, what little he'd seen of it. Always felt like tempting fate. Or welcoming the inevitable. Not once did he and Tomás ever come out of it with anything of value. He doubted it would change the next time Tomás suggested they try again.

The shift in energy as they passed the threshold of the forest and into a familiar world was enough to lift Ciarán's spirits. He'd never been so happy to be rained on and have it not be a dehydrated yellow. He ran his hand over his face, wiping away the slick dampness away from his eyes. "Heaven above, what a day. Time to find a pub?"

Tomás outturned his pockets. "We ain't got any coin left. Didn't think that gnome would steal my wallet, too." He flashed an accusatory glare.

"And that's my fault? Not like I could do nothin' when that little girl and her dragon launched us three ways to Sunday."

"Yer fault for leavin' yer wallet inside yer hook."

"What, am I meant to leave it in my pocket where an angry gnome can up and bludgeon us fer it?"

"Better'n getting my hook caught on a tree branch."

"Hey, that tree branch saved our lives!"

"And robbed us blind!"

"It was a *tree*, ya numpty! What's *yer* excuse for the gnome?"

"Oh, come off it, ya—"

"I beg your pardon, boys," a voice called from the side. "Apologies for interrupting your lovers' quarrel."

Ciarán shot his eyes to the left, catching sight of a plump man leaning against a horse-drawn wagon. He was dressed to the nines in expensive...everything. His wardrobe probably cost more than the entirety of Nóra. Beside him was a rube who appeared to be a retainer of some sort. Ciarán's instinct was to knock them both out cold and pilfer them for their coin and probably everything else on the noble's person. But then he made note of the guard's sword, and without his hook, he couldn't do much of nothing.

Then he noticed the sword had no...*sword* on it. But he also was far too tired and sore and demoralized from everything that had occurred over the last day.

Regardless, the noble did not wait for answer. He approached, his eager retainer staying at his side. He linked his fingers together, cleared his throat, and asked, "What was this I heard about a girl with a dragon?"

"Oh, my aching hook," Ciarán muttered.

Chapter Nineteen

"Honestly, how does someone not own a pan to cook in? What does he do, stick his hand in a fire?"

"A look at his left hand might answer that question. One time, when he was around eleven or twelve years old..."

The evening, much to Ailís's surprise and relief, had been proceeding wonderfully. An instant connection between her ma and Áine seemed to have been struck from the moment Áine unpacked her baking supplies and equipment—largely because Uncle Iósaf had no such tools of his own. Much of their laughter came at Iósaf's expense, and, without his presence to deter any embarrassing stories, Áine may have learned more than she needed or wanted to know about him.

Ailís stood off to the side, flour covering her hands and skirt, the kitchen having been upturned by a whirlwind of culinary chaos. Ma's head was reared back in laughter as she concluded a story revolving around Uncle Iósaf's experience with a hurling stick, a cast iron pan, a sprig of heather, and a book detailing the rise and fall and rise again of mercantilism and the grain economy. At some point Ailís lost where it had any connection to the Thrice-Eaten Feast of the Thrice-Dead Prophet of eight years past (she only loosely remembered the book). At least it made Áine grin as she rolled the fresh pie dough atop the baking tin.

Regardless, it was enough for Ailís to throw her hands on her hips and say, "Why does *she* get all these stories about Uncle Iósaf and *I* never have?" She pouted, though only facetiously.

Ma flashed a smile at her. "Ailís, one day, if you're lucky, you may get the chance to share embarrassing stories about *your* brother to a woman he has his eyes on."

"What?" Camaráin called from the other room. He was at the table, reading a book—as he always did—entitled, *Scaled in Flames: or How I Learned to Stop Worrying and Love the Grain Economy.* He had grabbed it from the library during a moment of quiet while Uncle Iósaf was catching his breath. After their uncle sent along his well wishes for happy reading and closed the door after Camaráin, he resumed his wailing.

"Don't worry about it, dear!" Ma said with a chuckle. She smirked at Áine, who only shook her head with a measure of evident annoyance.

Despite the teasing, Áine finished the pie without losing focus, crimping the top layer and carving a small vent in the center. The richness of the berries was already making for a delectable aroma. Into the oven it went, and already she returned to sprinkling more flour on the counter and rolling out a healthy amount of dough.

"How many pies are you gonna bake?" Ailís asked, her heart fluttering with anticipation. She folded her hands together and approached the counter, watching Áine intently as she attacked the dough with a rolling pin.

"How many do you want?" the woman responded. As Ailís's mouth began to open, Áine quickly added, "I'm not making *that* many. This is all dough I needed to use today, anyway. And, from the look of that basket over there—" She nudged her head to her right, where an assortment of root vegetables lay withering. "—I suppose I'm doing *him* a kindness, too."

"You're gonna put veggies in a *pie*?" Ailís asked, sneering.

"Not a pie. A tart."

"What's the difference?"

"Not a lot."

"Do tarts only use veggies and pies only use fruits?"

"Sure." Áine shrugged her shoulders as she continued rolling out the dough for the tart.

Ailís grunted in acknowledgment. "I think I'll just have the pie, then," she murmured.

Ma shook her head. "Don't be rude, Ailís. This kind woman is taking the time to bake for people she doesn't even know."

"And for Pilib!" Ailís added.

The dragon squawked at the mention of his name. A sudden clunk signaled his short-lived flight from the table, and his scales scratched against the floor as she slithered about until finding his way up Ailís's leg and atop her shoulder—quickly growing to be his favorite spot to perch. His tongue lolled out of his mouth as the kitchen was filled with all the various aromas. His eyes were locked on the counter, watching every movement of Áine's hands while she rolled out the dough.

"See! He can't wait for his party to start!"

"The dragon isn't the only one eating tonight, Ailís," Ma admonished. She inclined her head toward Áine, a warm smile on her face. "Thank you, Áine, for...indulging my daughter."

Áine swatted the air to deflect the comment and remained focused on the dough, which was now stretched across length of the counter. "Think nothing of it, Máirín. An egg hasn't hatched south of the Highlands and the Cliffs in ages; it's call for a celebration."

She seemed earnest in saying so. Not at all annoyed as Ma was. And yet, Ailís could not quite determine why Áine still sounded so morose when speaking of Pilib.

Before Ailís could raise the issue, Ma said, "Well, thank you, regardless. I'm impressed at, well...*everything* you've done here today."

"Yeah, you really know what you're doing more than Ma does!" Ailís said with a smile.

Ma shot her a glance, her brow furrowed.

"What? She does."

"You're having some of this tart before you get any pie, missy," Ma said, pointing to the still-unfilled pastry. "You still owe me a new baking tin, by the way."

Ailís's head hung low. "I'll just give the tart to Pilib while you're not looking."

"Then I won't take my eyes off you."

"But, then Pilib will go hungry!"

"He'll still get pie."

The dragon spread his wings, squawking and chirping his approval. A surge of excitement welled within him, primed and ready to burst—a sensation not at all lost on Ailís.

"Oh, quiet, you," Ailís said, scratching underneath his chin. "If I have to eat vegetables, then so do you."

Pilib hardly seemed to mind. Hearing the word "eat" appeared to be more than enough.

The ghost of a smile creased across Áine's face as she walked over to the vegetable basket and chopped those that looked usable and groaned with disgust at the ones bearing more the resemblance to a children's horror story monster.

When it came time for the festivities to begin, the various pies and tarts were brought out to the dining table. Ailís stared with mouth agape as Áine scurried back and forth between the kitchen and the dining room, a new pie in her hands each time she returned. Before she knew it, seven pies and tarts sat on the table, all baked perfectly with a flaky crust and filling the space with the most delicious aroma she had ever smelled. "How did you do all this?" Ailís asked.

"Would you believe me if I said, 'magic?'" There was an air of mystery lining Áine's words. The sly look in her eyes as she brought out *another* pie only exacerbated it.

Ailís leaned over to her brother, who had yet to look up from his book. "Cam, is there such a thing as pie magic in that book?" she whispered.

"I'll let you know if they get into it during the fall of the grain economy."

"Thanks."

As the (supposedly) final pie was brought out, Áine dusted the coating of flour off her palms and said, "Dig in."

Pilib needed no encouragement. The dragon leaped from Ailís's shoulder and splintered the wood of the table upon landing, but half of one of the vegetable tarts was devoured in an instant. He crooned his approval with a long trill, his head tilted back with what appeared to be a smile.

Idle conversations provided a backdrop for the sound of Pilib's scales scraping against the baking tins and the sloshing of berries and pie crust inside his mouth. Ma and Camaráin's awe at the ferocity with which the hatchling ate was countered by

Áine's calm disposition. It had distracted Ailís enough that she almost did not recognize that Uncle Iósaf had at last stopped wailing. She got up, chair legs dragging against the floor, and she nodded to her ma as she glanced at the closed library. After reaching the ornate door, her eyes drawn again to the strange etchings at the bottom, she rapped her knuckles against the wood and pressed an ear close. "Uncle Iósaf?"

A nondescript noise was the response, but it was at least *a* response.

"There's a lot of pie here. I don't think we'll finish it all."

Another succession of strange noises, but this time, Ailís got the gist of it.

"Yes, we convinced her to stay. She worked really hard."

More noise.

"We only talked a little bit about that burn on your hand... okay, more than a little bit."

This time, silence.

"You're gonna miss out on watching a dragon eat a pie in two bites!"

The door unlatched, and from the look of Uncle Iósaf...one would not have been able to tell he had spent the past few hours screaming his frustrations. For all the screaming and stomping and inane ramblings, Ailís expected him to have torn half his hair out and knocked all the books off the shelves. But he looked the same as he had when his heart dropped out of his pants at Áine's arrival (though his face was a shade or two redder), and the library actually *tidier* than it had a few hours ago.

Ailís held out her hand, gesturing for him to come to the table, but he refused it, holding up a palm in deference.

"I'm fine here," he said, leaning against the doorframe.

Looking back at her ma, Ailís shrugged and walked toward the table, to the promise of pie and the goal to avoid the vegetable tart, but she could not help but suck in a breath when she saw Áine approach, holding a plate with a slice of blackberry pie. Uncle Iósaf was already turning to retreat into the library.

Áine reached out and grabbed his hand before he could do so. Iósaf went rigid, but after a hesitation, turned to face her.

She held out the plate to him. "Hello," she said. "I'm Áine. It's nice to meet you."

Iósaf's lip quivered, his hands shaking. "Hello," he finally said, taking the plate. He seemed as surprised as anyone that he managed to say an actual word.

Ailís turned toward Camaráin with a grin and mouthed, "Pie magic."

Her brother held up his book and started waving it around, holding his thumb up.

Although Iósaf and Áine regarded one another in silence, it seemed a contented one, and one that Ailís could not help but smile at as the clinking of forks against plates continued to ring out in the background. It was a wonderful moment, a tender moment.

Naturally, it had to be ruined by Pilib belching.

Uncle Iósaf tried and failed to stifle a chuckle. Áine rolled her eyes.

Suddenly, the door crashed open, sending splinters loose onto the floor as it slammed against the walls. The vegetable stalks in the garden were still wavering when thumping foot-steps entered the room. Ailís could not see anyone past the table, but from the shadow cast by the candlelight and the agitated grunting, she knew Adhamh had just entered the house. Everyone stopped eating after the gnome's entrance except for Pilib, who, while trying to eat a pie in one bite, seemed to be competing with Adhamh to see who could make the most noise.

"Adhamh?" Iósaf said, inclining his head toward the gnome. "What is it?"

The gnome kicked over an empty chair and stamped on the floor, an unpleasant string of words escaping his mouth.

"Whoa! We still have guests here, Adhamh! You can't talk like that!"

Adhamh snapped off a chair leg and began beating it against the floor.

"I understand that, but that doesn't explain what that has to do with their mothers."

The chair leg was chucked across the room, and whatever escaped Adhamh's lips was either a long scream or the longest word in the fae language. It was enough to break Pilib from his pie-induced reverie.

"Oh," Iósaf said. "Well, when you word it like that..."

"Uncle Iósaf?" Ailís said, growing fearful of the gnome's rage. "What's wrong? Why is Adhamh so...?" She trembled, and Áine wrapped an arm around her shoulder.

"Huh?" her uncle said, his brow furrowed. "Oh, right, right." He pointed his thumb at the door. "We have some unwanted visitors. You all should hide or something."

Chapter Twenty

The room erupted into a whirlwind of chaos. Ma rushed toward Ailís while Camaráin grabbed Pilib and ran to the library. Adhamh continued his tirade of colorful fae slurs and Uncle Iósaf calmly ate his slice of pie.

"Uncle—" Ailís called, but Áine placed a hand over her mouth and Ma pushed her back into the library. Worry bore down on her chest as she reached out to him, helpless with all her lack of strength.

Yet, for all the anxiety of the moment, Iósaf's attention remained affixed to the pie on his plate. He nodded along with each bite, humming his approval, as though the panic he instilled in them did not matter to him. That, or he could not be bothered to be torn away from what was, truthfully, an excellent slice of pie.

Heavy footsteps thumped in the clearing as an entourage approached the cottage. Because of the small height of the door, Ailís could not see who waited on the other side of it—only that one member of the group of four had a plump lower half. Once Iósaf finished his dessert, he crouched under the door to greet the new arrivals, Adhamh following in tow.

Ailís felt safe enough to crane her head around the library

door, despite her ma's protests. Camaráin sat in a nearby chair with Pilib in his lap, and the dragon, in the midst of all the chaos, managed to grab another pie before he was carried off. If he was frightened, it didn't prevent him from eating.

"Can I help you, lads?" Iósaf called. His voice carried an unfamiliar icy tone.

Adhamh offered a greeting of his own that was probably far less friendly.

"Pardon me, my good man, I hope I am not interrupting." Ailís could hardly forget the haughty and pompous voice of Lord Saibhir. "Though, judging from the enchanting aroma, I assume I am indeed interrupting."

Iósaf grunted. "Indeed, you are."

"So many wondrous scents, though. Surely, you did not cook such a feast for yourself?"

"Why not? You seem to."

Ailís stifled her laughter.

"Besides," Uncle Iósaf continued, "*this* one eats like a cow. Don't underestimate a gnome's appetite. Could probably eat *you* under the table."

Adhamh stomped, pointed this way and that, and grumbled something that may have been an agreement, may have been an insult, or may have been some combination thereof.

"Hey, wait a tick!" one of the accompanying sets of legs shouted. "I recognize you!"

Her eyes widening, Ailís ducked behind the wall, gritting her teeth. "Whoops," she hissed under her breath, trying not to glance at what was surely her ma's glare of death. That voice was so familiar, too...

"You're that gnome what bludgeoned us!"

"Aye, and beat the piss out of us, too!" added a second voice.

"That's what 'bludgeoned' means, ya numpty!"

"Ah, come off it, Ciarán."

"Oh!" Ailís gasped.

"What?" Ma hissed. "Keep your voice down."

"Those are the thieves from the other night. The ones who tried to take Pilib!" Ailís peered around the threshold. "But why are they with Lord Saibhir?"

A strange noise escaped Adhamh. It may have been a laugh.

Iósaf hummed his acknowledgment. "You must be today's brigands who got my friend Adhamh all flustered."

"He weren't flustered!" the second brigand said. "He's just an angry sop!"

"Well, clearly you don't have much experience with interrupting a gnome while nature calls."

"No," the first voice—Ciarán—said, dejection lining his words. "We're well aware. Ain't the first time. Ain't be the last, neither." He grunted. It sounded like someone elbowed him in the belly.

"Silence, all of you!" Lord Saibhir interrupted, his voice echoing through the woods. "The less time I am to do with these brigands, the better, I must say. How *do* you ever deal with them, my good man?"

"I don't," Iósaf said. "They don't get past the guard dog."

Adhamh growled, though if it was at Iósaf or Saibhir, Ailís couldn't tell.

"Now, then," her uncle continued, "can I help you?"

"Hmm, I hope so. There is a girl of great import whom I seek. She has pilfered some...items that belong to me. Have you made note of anyone who does not belong in these woods?"

Ailís gulped, peering over at Pilib. The dragon had tipped the empty baking tin over his head and was wearing it like a hat. Crumbs were everywhere. Camaráin looked more distressed by the mess than by their present situation.

"You seem a long ways from home," Iósaf said. "I'm willing to guess she'd be far from home, too. And, what with all the spooky fae and angry gnomes about, I'd wager she would be a fool to hide in a place like the Crann Woods."

Lord Saibhir seemed to consider these words. "Are you an expert on matters of foolishness, sir, as a dweller of these woods?"

"A scholar on such matters, perhaps, but not an active participant."

"Oh, my, a scholar! Do you consider this hovel to be something of a field study, then?"

"No, I would daresay a 'sabbatical' would be the correct term. One is better equipped to learn in such quiet environs."

"One could not *live* in such *squalid* environs, sir! Only a fool would seek to thrive on such meager means."

"Perhaps it is only the fool who believes he needs anything *more* than but meager means."

"A fool has not lived in the lap of luxury."

"A fool is not aware that such luxury does not a joyous life make."

This went on. For a while. Ailís eventually grabbed a book and read through half of it. At one point, Áine went to the dining table and grabbed two of the remaining pies without drawing any attention from outside. Listening was hungry work.

"Very well, sir!" Lord Saibhir eventually said. "I will away. Come, brigands! She shan't have gone far. We have been delayed enough by such...foolishness."

The footsteps receded into the woods, and the front door finally shut. The distant sound of grumbling and curses indicated Iósaf had shut the door on Adhamh before he had a chance to enter.

Ailís shot to her feet, nearly dropping her pie. "Uncle Ióshaf!" she exclaimed, still working on half a bite, specks of purple spittle flying from her mouth. She swallowed her food before continuing. "Are you okay?"

Her uncle reached for the plate he left on the table and offered her a gentle smile, scratching at the back of his head. "You know, I was so wrapped up in you all sticking it to the Inquisition that it never registered with me that you said you had Lord Saibhir hot on your tails, too."

Ma crossed her arms as she regarded her brother. "Is that a problem?"

Frowning, Iósaf exchanged a glance with Áine and said, "Yeah, probably. We should...maybe try and get you out of here."

Chapter Twenty-One

"Wait, so you actually *know* Lord Saibhir?" Ma asked, throwing her hands out at her side. Tension rose in the room to match that of her voice.

Whatever happened in the library it didn't reach the dining room. Iósaf shrugged as he took another bite of his pie. "What, was he not our governor six years ago?"

"He's been our governor for most of our lives, Iósaf."

"Alright, alright. Just making sure."

"But, you *know* him? As in, *personally* know him?"

A dribble of blackberry juice trailed down from the corner of Iósaf's lip. He wiped at it and picked at the crumbs on his plate. "Oh yeah. I go way back with him." He suppressed a burp. "I hate the guy."

Ma drew Ailís closer to her. "You said we need to get out of here. Why?"

Ailís hummed her confusion. "Um, Ma? Remember how he was trying to find Pilib, and we got away before that happened? Maybe because of that?"

"Well, yes, Ailís, but you can say the same of the Inquisition."

Iósaf grunted.

"Iósaf?" Ma asked, raising an eyebrow. "Safe to say you feel differently there?"

He remained silent for a moment, punctuated only by Adhamh's persistent muttering outside. It was only when he gulped and sighed with relief that he moved again. "*Nngh*, sorry about that. Pie went down the wrong pipe."

"Are you okay?" Ailís asked, pushing past her ma and running to his side.

Waving his hand, Uncle Iósaf flashed a smile. "Oh yes, perfectly fine. Just...couldn't help myself." Even as pained tears were trickling down his eyes, he was already reaching for another slice of pie.

"So...what do we have to fear then?" Ailís inclined her head toward him, nervously scratching at her left arm. "He sounds just like an Inquisitor."

"What?" He scrunched his face together with confusion, his hand hovering over the nearest pie tin. "Oh, sorry, I don't think I was listening. No, Saibhir is *worse* than the Inquisition."

"Worse?" Ailís repeated.

"What, is he an Inquisitor with a brain, then?" Ma asked as she walked out of the library.

The question made Iósaf laugh. "Nah, he's dumber."

"And that makes him worse...how?"

Iósaf cleared his throat, massaging the outside of his neck with a grimace. "You ever meet a man who thinks himself above the law and untouchable? Someone who would try to steal the world and put it on display if he could?"

Ailís leaned closer to her mother and whispered, "Wait, we have laws? I thought you said you made those up?"

"I made up *those* laws, Ailís," Ma said. "*Those* ones didn't exist. We still have other laws. They're just not under the Inquisition's jurisdiction."

"And what a jurisdiction it is," Iósaf added, his voice rife with sarcasm. "Dumb as they are, at least they don't have anyone shirking the laws they have established. *That* is Lord Saibhir in a nutshell. I wouldn't be surprised if the man wrote into law, 'The Inquisition can't do anything to me.'"

"No one would be *that* stupid to try." Ma rolled her eyes.

"Oh, no, he *did* try. That's why I said I wouldn't be surprised."

Ailís couldn't help but be confused by that. She didn't understand politics: how it worked, how people used it, what purpose it served. All she was getting out of it was the rules were generally made up to suit whoever was writing them. She looked over at Áine, who appeared pensive in thought, listening intently to Iósaf's words. The purpose of politics seemed to perplex her, as well.

"How would you *know* that, though, Iósaf?" Ma asked. "That sounds like one of your dumb jokes."

Remaining uncharacteristically quiet Iósaf sighed. "I never explained...why I had to leave Baile, did I?"

Her breath catching, Ailís turned toward her uncle with quivering eyes, and squeaked out a meager, "No."

Ma's "no" was more forceful.

"Once upon a time, I thought of Saibhir as a...well, a colleague would be too strong a term. Acquaintance? Not really. Guy who also was interested in dragons? Yeah, that works. We were guys who were interested in dragons. I learned of his collection of draconic artifacts when I was sneaking into his mansion once for reasons not pertinent to this discussion, please do not ask any further questions, Máirín. We bonded over what I presumed to be an enjoyment of the truth long since veiled by the Inquisition. I was so enamored with the number of draconic fangs, scales, claws, and the like he had procured that I did not stop to think about the implications of it all. Not once did I stop to think about how he is probably the single reason why the draconic black market is as lively as it is—he keeps it all afloat himself. He doesn't care about the pursuit of knowledge; he cares only for having *things*. To him, these eggs are nothing more than a feather in a cap that should really not be adding any more feathers."

"But where do *you* play into all of this?" Ma asked, furrowing her brow.

Iósaf bunched his hand into a fist, and for the first time, Ailís saw what she surmised to be a pang of guilt in her uncle's eyes. "I can only blame myself. I didn't actively participate in the black market, but I did share so much of what I had learned about draconic lore. I can't help but think about what he used that knowledge for, what relics he sought because I mentioned they might exist. And when I had nothing more to share, he sold me out to the Inquisition." He grunted and reached for his pie again. His next bite was angrier than it had any right to be for eating something so delicious. "Heaven above, I was a fool. I should have been suspicious when I learned he was illiterate."

Everyone stopped and looked at Iósaf. Áine ceased her silent pondering, Pilib stopped squawking at Camaráin, Camaráin stopped squawking at Pilib, and even Adhamh had fallen quiet outside (though correlation did not necessarily indicate causation on that last one).

"Umm..." Ailís said, scratching at her head.

Her uncle kept on at his pie. It appeared to quell whatever

momentary anger he had. It also made him evidently oblivious. "So, yeah. I knew Lord Saibhir some years ago. He's the reason why I—"

"Back it up a moment, Iósaf," Ma said, holding up her hand. "Did you just say he's illiterate?"

Shrugging, Iósaf pressed on with his chewing, holding the fork out in one hand and the plate in the other. "Yeah? I had a bit of a laugh when I learned it. I mean, the man only has two books: neither have to do with dragons, one is that giant book by Warren Peace that he's used as a weapon, and the other's pages were used exclusively as toilet paper."

"Are you *serious*?" Áine muttered, aghast. For once, her incredulity did not seem directed at Iósaf.

"Look, I wouldn't have believed it either had I not seen it happen. Now, don't ask me why I was in his privy, but—"

"No," the woodland woman interrupted. "Not that. I just..." She turned away from the conversation, and her voice lowered as she murmured, "I can't believe it was to *him* that..."

Ailís craned her head. "Áine? What is it?"

The woman didn't respond, still apparently lost in her thoughts.

Ma threw her hands up in the air. "There's too much to unpack there, but should we not be concerned that he most likely recognized you?"

Loudly chewing, Iósaf shook his head. "Oh, no. He was far too amused by Adhamh to look at me. But still..." He took another big bite. "On the off chance he did remember me, my vote is to head to the Draconic Highlands."

He hummed with satisfaction. "And we're taking this pie with us."

Chapter Twenty-Two

Ever since she was a little(er) girl, Ailís had fantasized about the Draconic Highlands—what the Inquisition had hoped to hide beyond the Cliffs of Ard, what they refused to admit still existed beyond there, where they were. But they had ever remained just that: a fantasy. A remnant of stories told long ago by her uncle clashing with the histories the Inquisition acknowledged, but also didn't acknowledge, but still kind of did.

Now, though, those fantasies were becoming reality. A hatchling dragon was perched on her shoulder. She suddenly had come into powers she did not think were possible. Vegetables were being put into baked goods. Nothing was what it used to be.

It was not every day the opportunity presented itself to journey to the home of the dragons. Therefore, there was no better time for her to say, with the same energy as presenting an idea for a field trip, "Let's go to the Draconic Highlands!"

No one matched her enthusiasm. Áine remained lost in her own thoughts. Ma expressed utter incredulity at the suggestion. Uncle Iósaf switched his attention to the tart and muttered to himself about how good it was. Camaráin went back into the library to look at books. Pilib had passed out from a sugar crash.

It was not the response she was looking for. "Or...are we *not* going to?" Ailís furrowed her brow, looking for some inkling one way or the other. "Will we not be safe there?"

Ma redirected her focus on her brother rather than address Ailís's question. "Iósaf, have you even been to the Draconic Highlands?"

Driblets of crumbs and root vegetables tumbled out of the corner of Iósaf's mouth as he chewed. "Nah, can't shay I have."

"Do you know the *way*?" Ma flashed an annoyed sneer at him.

"Sure, everyone doesh." He swallowed his food, shrugging. "Just go through the Cliffs of Ard, yeah? Not too complicated."

"'Not too complicated?' Iósaf, these are the *Cliffs of Ard*. Don't you realize how treacherous they are?"

"Are you an expert on the area, Máirín?" Áine asked. She rested her hand on her chin, her striking eyes boring into Ma's. "I didn't think you had ever left your home village, no?"

Ma turned away, her nostrils flaring as she opened and closed her mouth in quick succession without producing any words. After a huff of breath, she managed to say, "Everyone knows that, Áine. Don't you know the rhyme? 'Cliffs of Tall, lest you fall. Cliffs of Small, lest you also fall. Cliffs that are Awaiting a Growth Spurt, look, just trust us, you're going to fall.' We've been taught...that..." She trailed off, shaking her head. "I guess I never said it out loud."

Áine smirked. "Even when you remain steadfast against the lies of the Inquisition, sometimes the lies are unavoidable." She drew a deep breath, closing her blue eyes. "It's an innocuous thing, isn't it? The dangerous roads leading through the Cliffs of Ard, a byway no one in their right mind would seek to traverse. When you know the Cliffs, you can't help but laugh about it." She pursed her lips, before opening her eyes and turning her focus on the sleeping Pilib. "All these deceptions, just to maintain the stories that they cannot keep straight. 'We vanquished the dragons, but also stay away from the Cliffs of Ard and don't ask any further questions.'"

The rant was the only thing keeping Iósaf from shoveling more pie in his mouth. She had his full attention.

"In reality," Áine continued, "the Cliffs are nothing but a paradoxical lie created by the Inquisition merely because they couldn't find their way past the barrier created by the dragons themselves, so they opted to shout, 'Forbidden land!' at the top of their lungs and called it a day. The wall that marks where the Cliffs end and the Highlands begin was not only one to prevent the dragons from ever being rediscovered, but also to forget they existed to begin with."

"Wait," Ailís said, stepping toward the woman. "What do you mean, 'the barrier created by the dragons themselves?' I don't understand."

A weary smile stretched across Áine's lips. She held up a fist and said, "Air, water, earth, fire." With each word, she raised a finger. "The four elements that bind our world. You may be aware of them already—storytellers tend to find a way to put them in their tales, somehow. But here in our world, the dragons can be considered...guardians of these elements, in a sense. Of water, to maintain the purity of our oceans and lakes and rainfall. Of fire, to provide us all with life-giving warmth. Of air, to ensure the safety of that which we breathe. Of earth, to see to the health of our crops and our land...and sometimes, to erect a natural barrier to avoid the idiocy of the Inquisition."

"A power move," Ma muttered under her breath.

Áine nodded. "That it was. Sometimes I wish for the same." She chuckled. "And with whom a dragon sought to bond was based on the elements they championed. Water dragons wished for partners of great passion. Fire dragons sought those brimming with vitality and courage. An earth dragon would look for one with such inner strength befitting the land itself." With a pause, her gaze lingered on the young pair. "You're an imaginative and insightful girl, Ailís. A perfect bond for an air dragon such as Pilib. I'm sure he could sense it straight away."

The remark had Ailís reaching for the hatchling, even as he continued to sleep. She cradled him in her arms, the sharpness of his scales digging into her skin. "You already knew this," she said, not as an acknowledgment to Áine's words, but as a confirmation to herself. "That's why you didn't get scared when you first saw Pilib. But why did you always look so sad? *Why* do you know all this, Áine?"

A plate clattered on the dining table. Iósaf walked forward, his eyes focused on the collection of tomes in his library.

The focus of his attention did not seem lost on Áine. She nodded. "Precisely so."

Ailís raised a confused eyebrow. "What's 'precisely so?' What is it?"

Iósaf chuckled, first in disbelief, then with joy. "She's a Draconic Priest."

"*Was* a Draconic Priest," Áine corrected. "I'd wager I'm one of the few left. Maybe the only one left."

"Unbelievable," Iósaf muttered. He gestured a shaking hand toward the library. "I feel like I should offer these back to you."

The woman was quick to shake her head. "No, no. I...thank you, but no. I fear they would only bring back bad memories. Of the days when our lives secreted deep in the valleys of the Cliffs of Ard were betrayed by one of our own, an opportunist who found smuggling to be a more worthwhile option. He would rather have seen the High Inquisitor put our order to the torch just to escape us in the chaos of it all. It perplexed us all—we weren't forcing him to stay there. But now he's off to who-knows-where, while I escaped with my life to bake pies in the woods for faeries and gnomes. Sometimes, how things end up don't make much sense."

"They don't need to make sense," Ailís said, clutching Pilib. "It meant we got to meet you. It meant you got to meet Pilib."

The dragon snorted in his sleep, evidently having an eventful dream.

A tear trickled down Áine's face, and she quickly batted it away. "Perhaps it's fate, then. Or just coincidence, I don't know. I had planned to drink some wine and go to bed early tonight. Either way, I'll lead you through the Cliffs of Ard. Not like I have anything else going on."

Chapter Twenty-Three

The Crann Woods looked different at night. The fae eyes continued to lurk and watch, the rustling in the trees continued. Pinpricks of light wisped along in the boreal shadows, following their every step. The darkness was heavy, denser, and seeming to take on a life of its own among the fae.

All that to say, Ailís was bloody terrified.

She clutched her ma's wrist with enough force to dig her nails into her skin. Off to her left, Camaráin was doing the same to her. Within her bag, Pilib was fast asleep. It was a frightening time for all.

All, save for Iósaf and Áine. The two forest dwellers remained well ahead of the rest of them, undeterred by the chilling scene. When they had first set out from Iósaf's cottage, Ailís had asked, "What if one of the faeries eats us?" Despite her uncle's previous assurances that those ambiguous tales of the trickery of the fae were overblown at best, those concerns could not be prevented from reemerging when faced with faeries of the nocturnal persuasion.

To assuage her worries, Iósaf had responded, "What if they do what now?" And that was the end of that discussion.

The longer they walked through the the dark forest, the

more Áine seemed to be cognizant of Ailís's fears. She constantly looked back, offering a comforting smile where she could (such that the shadows would allow), but even she seemed reticent to say anything.

Was she also apprehensive of what lurked in the dark? Ailís noticed the woman did not move with the same confidence as her uncle did. But her uncle also didn't do much of anything with the same what-have-you as anyone else.

Not even when the eyes in the shadows grew frantic was he broken from his reverie. Against the backdrop of these illuminations turning their attention away from the family, Iósaf turned, the light on his face fading as the eyes moved further and further away, and with a wave of his arm, he said, "Shouldn't be much longer now! Heaven above, I can't wait to get some fresh air." His voice was startling. It was the first noise Ailís had heard beyond the ambient sounds of the forest in what felt like hours.

Despite her uncle's cheer, Ailís could not help but feel a sense of dread. She wrapped herself around her ma's arm, dragging her brother along with her. "Can we please leave?" she asked, her voice shaking. "Please?"

Iósaf's face was enshrouded in darkness, but the vague shape of his arm waving them along signaled his presence. "I told you there's nothing to worry about, didn't I? I won't let anything happen to you. I promise."

The trees began to rustle, leaves and twigs snapping.

"The hell was that?" Iósaf's sudden change in tone made them all alert

Áine crouched, quickly looking from one direction to the next. "Iósaf, I don't think we're alone in here."

"We're *well* past that!" Ailís shouted. Ma's quieting hand quickly clasped over her mouth, as it was wont to do.

Camaráin ducked behind her, clutching his bag close to this chest.

As the rustling drew nearer, Iósaf and Áine pushed their way in front of the others, barring them from whatever was approaching.

"If it comes down to it," Iósaf said, "run."

"Run where?" Ailís said, muffled by her ma's hand.

Iósaf flashed her a perplexed look. "*North.*" His tone indicated that should have been obvious. "Where we've been headed?" He leaned closer to Áine—which would have been unthinkable just a few hours previous—and whispered just loud enough for Ailís to hear, "We *have* been heading north, right?"

"Oh, sweet mercy," Áine and Ma muttered. They both buried their faces in their hands.

The footsteps grew louder, and with them, voices. A group of them. The fae eyes were buzzing with anticipation. Arguments overlapped with one another. Faeries crossed the clearing with their arms outstretched, one of them screeching for reasons beyond Ailís's comprehension. She already had one leg half-turned to the north, ready to run when the situation called for it. Tiny tremors shook the earth, a twig falling from overhead, the voices drawing nearer, nearer, nearer.

"Get ready," Iósaf hissed, releasing his hold on Ailís. Whatever approached, he seemed ready to face it head-on.

A group rushed out from the wooden depths and tripped over each other's feet, collapsing atop one another in the middle of the pathway. Enough light was cast from the fae eyes to reveal a plump man with three slimmer people piled atop him.

The tension surrounding Iósaf vanished. "Oh, it's just these guys again. Never mind." The fae watchers dispersed and returned to their spots amongst the trees.

Her curiosity piqued, Ailís peered around her uncle and saw those familiar faces again: Lord Saibhir, one of his guards, and the two brigands who had tried to steal Pilib. She rolled her eyes.

"Get *off* me, you lowlifes!" Saibhir bellowed.

"None of us are on you," the hook-nosed thief said.

Saibhir bore the appearance of a turtle on his back, the way he was rocking back and forth. None of his companions—attendants or otherwise—seemed inclined to assist him. Eventually, he found his way back to his feet, dusting the dirt and leaves and twigs from his lavish adornments. "I must say, if never I have to traverse these accursed woods again, it will be too—who the devil are you all?" He only just noticed the family watching him. He puffed out his chest and threw his hands on his hips.

"Um, sir?" his guard said, resting his hand atop the area where a sword hilt would have been helpful. "You don't recognize that man?" He gestured toward Iósaf. "We just spoke with him."

"Oh, yes, of course!" Saibhir responded with a cough, muttering something that indicated he would not have recognized Iósaf had it not been pointed out to him. "How fortuitous to have encountered a friendly face after these long days."

"We saw each other about two hours ago," Iósaf said, shaking his head.

"Did we now? I fear it is so difficult to tell in these disorienting environs." The man scoured his eyes over the rest of those gathered before him. "Though I do not recall so many being in your company when last we met."

"Yeah, they were in the can."

"The 'can?'"

"That'd be the...facilities, Lord Saibhir," the guard said.

"Really? All of them at once, then?" The lord stroked his chin(s).

Iósaf shrugged. "I warned them not to eat my cooking."

"And yet, they seem quite alright now. Such a quick recovery is unheard of—trust me, I am quite experienced in that regard!" He barked a laugh.

"Eww," Ma muttered, her nostrils flaring with a sneer.

As Saibhir ceased his laughter, patting his stomach to a stop, he hummed to the tune of suspicion. "To traverse these woods at so late an hour is cause for concern. I would be remiss not to think of the safety of these fae folk, lest you be party to brigandry."

Ailís mouthed a confused, "What?" as she glared between Iósaf and Áine at the two thieves accompanying Saibhir. She grumbled in silence, though a strange sensation began to flare within her as Pilib woke up within the bag and started grumbling for violence.

"Therefore," Saibhir continued, "I must ask your reasons for being out at such a late hour."

Iósaf held out his hands. "Last I checked, there were no laws against wandering about at night."

"But think of these suspicious fae eyes being cast upon you. Should I not put their hearts at ease?"

"We don't need to answer anything of you," Ma barked. She

wrapped her arm around Ailís's shoulder and held her tight. "And you have no right to question us without a proper writ permitting you to do so!"

Ailís leaned in close. "Ma, what are you doing?" she whispered. "You said those don't exist."

"Taking a gamble," Ma responded through gritted teeth.

An exasperated sigh escaped Saibhir's lips. "What is it with people demanding these 'writs'? Things were so much easier a week ago. Paper!" He held out his hand, and his guard produced a flimsy sheet out of nowhere. The lord reached into his pocket and produced a quill and scribbled something on it. "See?" He held it out. "*Here's* your writ of questioning! Now, then, for what purpose—"

"There isn't even anything written on that!" Ma pointed a finger at what was still a blank sheet of paper. "You didn't put any ink on the quill, and we all know you're illiterate!"

"Hey!" Saibhir pointed right back at Ma. "I am no longer illiterate. Last week, I read *Mr. Dragon Meets His Grave*!"

"That's a picture book for babies. It has five words in it."

"And I read them all!"

"If I may, my lord," the guard whispered. "I recognize that woman. She's from Baile."

"Hey!" the previously hook-handed man shouted, pointing at the group with the arm where there used a hook-hand. "I saw her while she were sleepin'! That didn't come out right." He cleared his throat and peered through the gap between Iósaf and Áine. "And her!"

Ailís's eyes went wide. "Eep."

"That's the girl what has the dragon!"

"Eep!"

All joviality and care vanished from Saibhir's face. "Give it to me," he growled.

Pilib began scurrying within Ailís's bag before leaping out with wings spread, a triumphant emergence to instill fear in these blaggards' hearts—if he didn't immediately crash to the ground.

A sinister smile stretched across Saibhir's lips. "Excellent. I must thank you for your—"

"Now, Ailís!" Uncle Iósaf shouted.

When first she had summoned her newfound powers, Ailís was frightened. At the time, she had no idea what was happening to her, even though she had saved Pilib. Now, though, she knew there was nothing to fear. And as Pilib looked up at her, his eyes wide, every bit of his face reminding her of the newborn he still was, she felt no hesitation.

She pushed past her uncle, shouted, and swung her arms upward, casting a wide arc of wind from within the earth—which many scholars of the time would have argued was the origin of the wind—and smiled as she caught those brief moments of recognition upon Saibhir's face. The fear, the calls for a reprieve, the scream.

In an instant, Saibhir, along with his guard and the two brigands, were swept away in the gust, flung high above the trees to who knows where. All that remained of them was the voice of the once-hook-handed man shouting, "Ah, not again!"

Ailís sighed with relief. The watchful eyes of the fae flickered. She turned to face her family, taking in the proud and approving glances from her ma and uncle, and the adoration of her brother. Her dragon only seemed to want to sleep.

But Áine was less impressed. If anything, she was concerned.

"Huh. I didn't realize you knew how to do that. We should get you to the Highlands before you need to...do that again."

Chapter Twenty-Four

A sense of accomplishment filled Liam as he stared at the dense arboreal barrier of the Crann Woods. He had traveled all this way north from Baile in the company of High Inquisitor Dónal, and not once did he want to bury his head in the dirt in hope of release from this mortal coil. It was hard not to smile at that.

Despite the High Inquisitor's appearance, the man kept up well with his pace, stopping only for requisite snack and bodily breaks, and only three nap times. Liam had argued for one-and-a-half, but relented when he realized he was not actually consciously walking at one point, but sleepwalking.

Regardless, they made good time. Planting his hands on his hips, Liam glanced over at Dónal and asked, "Have you ever been inside the Crann Woods, High Inquisitor?"

"Nah, lad," Dónal said, shaking his head. "Much too humid for my tastes." He patted his palm along his breastplate.

"'Too humid?' What if you're chasing someone who escapes into these woods?"

"Well, then I suppose they'd win that round."

"You realize we are chasing after someone who could very well be in these woods, yes?"

"I should have said something earlier. I apologize."

"Why don't you just take the armor off?"

Dónal cleared his throat, his round cheeks growing red. "I must admit...I do not tend to wear anything under—"

"Oh, Heaven above," Liam muttered, glancing skyward for any sort of divine assistance. A sudden gale knocked him off balance for a moment, his hair flowing free in the brief breeze. He looked at the High Inquisitor, fully aware of the anger flaring in his eyes. "Well, then, short of the great fortune of the man just falling into our laps, I'd say our arrangement ends here."

The trees rustled and produced a strange, humanlike scream, multiplied by four. Above, there was a crash and crunch in the branches, followed by a series of heavy grunts. Liam looked up and spotted four men dangling in the branches, all groaning, but unharmed.

It was hard not to make note of the presence of Lord Saibhir among their number.

"Well, look at that," the High Inquisitor said, pointing to the branches above. "What great fortune."

Liam stared at the sky, dumbfounded. "Thank you, Prophet of Multiple Fatal Misfortunes?"

Above, Saibhir scrambled in a panic, huffing and puffing and clutching his chest. He turned, spotted Liam and Dónal on the ground, and pointed at them. "You, there! Boys! What day is it?"

"'What day is it?'" Liam repeated.

Dónal grunted. "You know, we never did establish a calendar of days. It would have made things easier."

Liam blinked at him. "It's Sunday, Dónal. As it is every seventh day."

"Huh, curious. We were meant to create a new system of days to replace the Monday to Sunday, but I suppose we left it on the backburner for too long."

"The backburner after what? Shortening your name?"

"Ah, I knew there was something else I was forgetting..."

Saibhir continued to flail overhead. "Just what *are* you churls muttering about? Can you not see I am trapped up here? Get me down this instant!"

Liam placed his hands on his hips and sneered at the man.

"Hold there," Saibhir said, his voice wavering with fear as the branches buckled beneath him. "Where have I seen you before?"

"Oh, me?" He turned toward the High Inquisitor and dug through his pockets, ignoring Dónal's yelp that was at first startled, but then curious and calm. The fake writ of arrest unfurled in his hand, dancing in the breeze. "Do you recognize this, my Lord?"

"Boy, I can't read," the lord responded, shrugging his shoulders as gingerly as the trees would allow. "...That," he added with haste. "I can't read that in...this light."

Liam grunted and held the scribbled "Arest him" up to Dónal's face. "High Inquisitor, did we not agree that there was no validity to this writ of arrest on a number of grounds—chief among them being that such a writ does not exist?"

"Aye, that is true, lad," Dónal affirmed. "Not to mention, under the jurisdiction of the Inquisition, we—"

"Fantastic, thank you." Liam crumpled the piece of paper and stamped it into the ground. "But do you not think it curious to find Lord Saibhir here after all?"

The High Inquisitor remained lost in thought, murmuring about just what the Inquisition's jurisdiction covered. It took a snap of Liam's fingers to regain his attention. "Ah, yes, how very curious." He leaned closer and whispered, "Why is it curious?"

"Something—or some*one*—brought him here, don't you think?"

"Ahh," Dónal said, tapping his forefinger against his lips. "I understand." He did not understand.

"Therefore," Liam continued, "I think we would not be outside our bounds to assume something of a...draconic nature drew Lord Saibhir here."

"Hmm, yes. Quite draconic, indeed."

"And, if we were to investigate on our own...I fear Lord Saibhir may get in our way."

Dónal stared at the sputtering lord for a long while. A smile stretched across his face, his mind working so hard Liam could almost see the sparks flying from his temple. "You're saying we should break his legs."

"What?" Liam questioned, aghast. "No. I'm not a monster. I was just going to leave him up there."

"Oh." Dónal sounded disappointed. "That's fine, too."

Gesturing to the opening to the Crann Woods, Liam said, "After you then, High Inquisitor."

Dónal nodded and took a few clanking steps forward, entering the woods with a groan. "Ugh, so humid. Lad, help me with my breastplate!"

With a shudder, Liam followed after the High Inquisitor, but not before showing his teeth at an increasingly flabbergasted Lord Saibhir on the way. "Bye-bye, now. A shame I cannot 'arest' you myself, but this will have to do."

It was only when they had spent five minutes in the woods, with Saibhir's shrill warnings of "cannibalistic fae" and "wicked magic" and "an angry gnome" echoing throughout, that Liam had a grim realization, stopping dead in his tracks, much to Dónal's confusion.

"He didn't get the joke. He couldn't...hear that I was saying 'arrest' like how he spelled it." He frowned, looking back to the shaking branches down the way. "Do we have time to explain it to him?"

Chapter Twenty-Five

Ailís didn't expect such a rush in leaving the Crann Woods, but from the moment she sent Lord Saibhir and his coterie to Heaven-knows-where, Áine was insistent on reaching the Draconic Highlands without a moment's rest.

Once they crested from the forest and into the northern plains, nary a word was spoken. No one had the breath to spare for one, what with the effort required to keep up with the former priest's pace. It barely permitted Ailís to appreciate the beauty of the world beyond the Crann Woods. This so-called "forbidden land" barred from entry by the Inquisition. Such a title implied a land of horror—and some of her school books sanctioned by the Inquisition, like *The Forbidden Land: The Stuff of the High Inquisitor's Nightmares* and *A Realm of Horrors: This Is Really Dragon Along*, were more explicit in the assertion—but in reality, the north was far more gorgeous than anything south of the Crann Woods.

The Cliffs of Ard loomed on the horizon, reaching to the sky like skinny fists. The sound of crashing waves echoed over the empty expanse, while the plains ahead were of the most vibrant green Ailís had ever seen. There was nothing to suggest this land ought to be forbidden territory, other than the rickety wooden signs planted in the ground that read, "Do not enter," and then, "Seriously! Turn around!" and then, "Forbidden land!" and finally, "**IF YOU VALUE YOUR LIFE PLEASE TURN AROU**"—it was clear they ran of space on the board.

It was only when Camaráin fell, short of breath, that the forced march was made to stop. "Áine!" Ma shouted, cradling her son as he rediscovered his breath. "I think we can afford ourselves a rest."

Exasperated, Áine planted her hands on her hips and nodded. Though she appeared disinclined to show it, she was out of breath, as well.

"What's the rush?" Iósaf asked, not meeting Áine's eyes. "Thanks to Ailís, we have at least a full day on Saibhir before we're safe past the Highlands!"

Sweat dripping down her brow, Áine raised a hesitant and shaking finger and pointed it at Ailís, who clutched Pilib tight in her grasp. "It's not Saibhir I'm worried about. It's her."

Ailís ran her hand against Pilib's cold scales, the dragon trilling with delight at her touch. He seemed unaware of Áine's concerns. "What do you mean?" she asked. "I can protect us! You don't have to worry about a thing."

"It's not for us that I worry, Ailís. I worry for *you.*"

"For me?" She lifted Pilib up to her shoulder, the hatchling's head hanging slack over it. As the dragon weighed on her, a pang of equivalent concern wavered through her. "Is my...bond with Pilib going to hurt me? Uncle Iósaf said it wasn't anything to worry about! That it's a natural thing the Inquisitors took from us!" She stared at her uncle, searching for his affirmation. He answered with a quiet nod.

Áine nodded as well. "And it is. The issue is less the bond

and more, well...more that you're so young."

A quizzical grunt rumbled in Iósaf's throat. "I've never read anything about there being any danger in bonding a dragon to someone of her age."

"I suppose there isn't a danger as such," Áine admitted. "The bond is established from the moment of hatching, and when held by the right person. Clearly, Ailís and Pilib were meant for one another, but the issue is more of a...historical concern."

"What, did she set a new record or something?" It was difficult to determine whether Iósaf's question was in jest or one of interest. "Trying to maintain one of those records that's not a real record because everyone cheats to maintain it?"

Her expression marked with confusion, Áine let her mouth fall agape and stared at Iósaf. "What are you even talking about?"

Before Iósaf could go off on whatever tangent he intended, Ma spoke up. "Ignore him. The historical context—what does that mean?" She ran her fingers through Camaráin's hair as the boy rested his eyes, clutching the strap of his bag with notable vigor.

Áine smacked her lips, her eyes remaining on Ailís. "Do you know how the Inquisition began?"

Furrowing her brow, Ailís stood. "Well, yes." She pointed at her uncle. "Uncle Iósaf told us the story. First Inquisitor Peadar challenged our relationship with the dragons and then was eaten and risen as a martyr."

"Yes," Áine nodded. "But did he also tell you the that First Inquisitor's actions were driven by grief?"

"Grief?"

"Yes." The priest grimaced. "Over his son."

Ailís gasped. A chill ran through her as Pilib tensed in her arms. The dragon rested a clawed foot on her shoulder as though he, too, wished never to let her go.

Áine looked to the northern horizon. "The First Inquisitor was from this area, originally, as were many of those born to bond with dragons. Peadar had a son, somewhere between Ailís and Camaráin's ages. He bonded with an air dragon—whether intentionally or no, it is not for me to say—and came into his bonded magic quickly. Without the proper training, discipline, and patience, he could not control his abilities and launched himself into the horizon, beyond the view of the Cliffs of Ard. Peadar would never see him again."

Ma looked down at Camaráin, who seemed to be sleeping soundly. "He lost his son and blamed the dragons for it."

"Grief can consume us. It certainly consumed Peadar." Áine sighed. "Enough for him to challenge the great Ollepheist about it."

Iósaf huffed an intrigued breath. "I don't think I've heard the name."

Áine nodded. "The true names of dragons have been lost to history, known only to the Draconic Priests. I'd wager even Pilib has a true name—sorry to say, Ailís."

The girl frowned. Pilib—or whatever his name was—snorted.

"But Ollepheist—such that the dragons have any hierarchy—is considered a monarch among them."

"'Is' considered?" Iósaf asked. "Then he's still..."

"Oh, yes. I'd imagine he still lives. Do you think we, in our meager existences, can do anything to harm a dragon? Nonviolent though they are, a dragon could crush us without a second thought."

"And the First Inquisitor was crazy enough to challenge him."

Another nod, as Áine grunted in acknowledgment. "As I said, grief can consume us. And Ollepheist has always been known for his short temper. Peadar picked a fight with the wrong dragon." She paused, scoffed, and shook her head, a smirk stretching across her face. "If he only waited about half an hour before challenging an annoyed dragon."

"What do you mean?" Ailís asked.

"Oh, his son was fine. It just took him a while to get home. He *did* launch himself quite a ways away."

Ailís's mouth dropped open. What sadness she felt toward the First Inquisitor's loss vanished and was replaced with disbelief. She removed Pilib from her shoulder and placed him on the ground. "So, if the argument between Ollepheist and Peadar had happened thirty-five minutes later, the Inquisition would never have happened?"

"Well, I think it'd be naïve to say it would have *never* happened. We as humans always run the risk of ruining everything for everyone by being stupid. But in this case, that kerfuffle could have been avoided. Instead, Peadar's son returned home, his father's blood still on Ollepheist's teeth, and he was understandably cross. The Inquisition began in earnest after that. It could have been stomped in an instant had Ollepheist not been consumed by his own guilt and opted to lead his brethren beyond the Cliffs of Ard in order to avoid further bloodshed. Though that makes for less of a heroic story on the part of the Inquisitors, but good stories travel well among those who know no better."

"Some of us knew better," Iósaf muttered, crossing his arms. "Just not enough."

Ailís stared at Pilib, his curious face returning it with his open-mouthed smile-resemblant. "So, you're worried I might start a new Inquisition? Do you think I'm not disciplined enough for Pilib? Is it because I don't listen to Ma most of the time?"

"Discipline with regards to listening to your mother is one thing," Ma said, rolling her eyes. "But discipline with regards to a power none of us have known for generations? That's another matter entirely." She looked at Áine. "Isn't it?"

With a sigh, Áine agreed. "She's right, Ailís. If it was a matter of separating you and Pilib of your bond, that would be one thing—but that's not possible at all. And so, for your safety, you should be trained with one of the draconic lorekeepers in the Highlands."

"Trained?" Ailís repeated.

"Lorekeepers?" Uncle Iósaf's eyes lit up.

"For how long?" Ma added. There was measured panic in her voice.

"The lorekeepers are quite what you expect," Áine said. "Scholars, such as the Priests were. Just...well, they're dragons. They were the ones responsible for training those with their bonded magic until they come of age."

Ma stood, gently resting Camaráin's head on the ground. The boy did not stir, despite all the commotion. "And when would she 'come of age?'"

The question hung in silence. All Áine could do was shrug. "It was different for each person. But, per the lorebooks and records, training the bonded will always take, at minimum..."

She paused, looking at the ground as she sighed. "A few years. It may be more for Ailís, given her age. But it also may be less. There's no way to know until, well, we know."

Her lip quivering, Ailís balled her hands into fists and looked at her Ma. Whatever apprehension she felt, she could tell it was matched in her ma's heart. "I'd get to stay with the dragons, though?"

Áine nodded.

"But what about Ma? And Cam?"

"Ailís..."

Ma remained silent. Camaráin stayed asleep.

"Traditionally..." Áine said with a sigh. "Separation is...req uired. The bond between the dragon must be stronger than between the family.

"But she's my daughter!" Ma shouted. "How will I know she is safe?"

For all the annoyances she had provided her ma over the years, there was a small part of Ailís that had thought Ma would relish the day she was out of the house. She was surprised at her reluctance to let her go. After all, someone had to make her day difficult, and Camaráin was too quiet to fill those shoes.

"I'll watch her."

Ailís and Ma both shot their eyes at Iósaf.

A tentative smile was on his lips, the breeze wafting his hair along. "If it's a matter of there not being a conflicting strong bond, but we still want someone to ensure she remains well...then I would think our bond has been distant enough these past six years for it not to interfere."

Ma did not respond, but tears streamed down her face.

"Think of it as me making up for lost time. My self-banishment has come to an end." Iósaf put his hands on his hips, channeling every image of the triumphant hero Ailís had read about.

Áine, though, was less convinced. "You just want to meet the lorekeepers."

Iósaf shrugged. Guilty as charged. "Two things can be true."

Chapter Twenty-Six

Somewhere in the world lay a mountain range that reached to the sky like a field of daggers. The ocean crashed against it, reaching forward with its icy grip, threatening to take hold those who would endeavor to pass through. To fall from such a height, it would be an endless descent yielding no end and promising no landing.

Such were descriptions that did *not* describe the Cliffs of Ard.

The remainder of the walk to the Cliffs was punctuated in silence. But it was a different sort which gripped them, separate from that rush of anxiety ensnaring them as they departed the Crann Woods. One could say it was a silence of three parts, but speaking was a different matter from delivering the same. It was safer to say it was a silence of a single part, and that part was sadness.

As Áine led the group through the winding pathways cutting through the Cliffs of Ard—a road bearing neither the treachery nor danger the Inquisition had promised—Ailís clasped her ma's hand, her lips quivering. Words were left unspoken—and it was better kept that way, for Ma did not take kindly to Ailís's first words since their departure being, "All I wanted was to throw Pilib a birthday party."

Despite having been given two birthday parties in his first few days of existence, Pilib matched Ailís's sadness, his head lolling from her bag, bumping along her thigh with each step.

In another time, Ailís would have appreciated the natural beauty of the cliffs flanking them with each step. The Cliffs of Ard glistened with ocean spray, and the seldom-trodden pathway shone in a vibrant green that grew only more verdant the further they traversed. Though there was, in truth, little to behold, it was nonetheless beautiful, a fact that could not be denied by the glittering sea to their right and the chirping gulls depositing food into one another's mouths to their left.

The trek in silence offered Ailís ample time to think. She found it difficult to look up at her ma. Pilib's scales ran cold against her touch. Camaráin trailed behind them, remaining ever vigilant of the safety of his messenger bag, the contents of which he was still reticent to share. This was her family, the only one she had ever known. And yet, in a few days, this little creature hanging from her bag had changed everything. Was it a punishment? Was it fate? Was it coincidence? She hadn't expected her story to be rife with such danger and consequence. She had just wanted to have fun with a dragon, as many would have, had their perceptions not been sullied by the Inquisition's ever-watchful eye and semi-literate hand.

And when loomed ahead the tall, jagged stone wall that marked the end of the Cliffs of Ard and the beginning of the Draconic Highlands, Ailís's heart began to thump, thump, thump. Would her spirits be lifted once again on the other side of the wall? Would it not be so scary? Would she at last be safe to laugh and play and love with her dragon?

As the Highlands came into view, Áine raised a hand, signaling a welcomed stop. Everyone took the opportunity to sit, save for Uncle Iósaf, who walked closer to the wall the drive to inspect it evidently all too enticing.

Ailís rested her head against Ma's arm, drawing a deep sigh. Pilib mimed the motion, right down to the sigh, and Camaráin sat cross-legged in front of them, quiet as always but a frown marring his normally introspective face. The sensation of weightlessness filled Ailís's limbs—perhaps Pilib trying to do *something* to comfort her—but she felt empty, regardless.

No one spoke until Uncle Iósaf returned, hands on his hips, and called out, "Well, this has gotten depressing."

Ma stared daggers at him.

He shrugged. "Well, it has."

"Sit down, Iósaf," Áine muttered, shaking her head.

Iósaf opened his mouth to speak further, but huffed a sigh and relented, plopping himself down and folding his hands in his lap. "I'm sorry," he said. "I...my own goodbye was sudden. I'm sure it wasn't easy for you all."

"That's putting it mildly," Ma murmured.

"But," Iósaf continued, "all the more reason this doesn't need to be as difficult now. I'll be with her. She won't be alone."

Ailís showed her uncle a wan smile, but she could manage little more than that. "Thank you," was all she said.

Pilib trilled with indifference, his eyes shutting. He could also have been bored. There had been far more excitement in his first few days out of the egg than there had been since they left the Crann Woods.

Iósaf seemed to realize he couldn't bring any levity to the moment. He offered a comforting smile and turned back toward the Highland wall. "Do you know how to get past it, Áine?" he asked.

Áine frowned. "I've never been beyond the wall, but there were tomes the Priests left behind which detailed proper passage into the Highlands. There are some sort of markers we'll need to keep an eye out for, but...hard to describe. I'll know them when I see them."

They had their destination in mind, then. The knowledge of it hung in the air between them, ready to grasp at a moment's notice.

But no one displayed eagerness to do so. For Ailís, to stand back on her feet, to resume their march toward what lay beyond the wall separating the Highlands from the rest of Nóra, would be to begin the long goodbye that would separate *herself* from the rest of Nóra. From Ma, from Camaráin. From her home and all the activities she cared not to take part in, from her dancing lessons and the fear instilled in her by Miss Róisín. Strange though it was, she found herself missing the concept of that. Just the concept, not the actual practice of it.

She couldn't surmise what reasons had ensnared everyone else, but they remained silent. It was only when Ma smacked her lips, rapping her fingers along Ailís's shoulders, that whatever barrier preventing their onward march began to fracture. "Well," she said, her voice weak. "Shall we?"

The moment they rose to their feet, a deep voice echoed over the valley. "Yes, and shall we join you?"

Ailís spun on her heel, trying—but failing—to shove Pilib into her bag. The dragon swatted her hand away by the force of his head. She yelped as she sneered at the hatchling, but then eyed two figures approaching from around the bend.

One was donned in the armor of the Inquisition, though with a flare of regality the others among his number did not display. It was offset by his otherwise disheveled state.

The other wore muddied and common rags that had grown threadbare in the elbows and knees. They fit well with his likewise disheveled physical appearance.

Ailís recognized he of the rattier clothing as the merchant from whom she rescued Pilib—despite his assertions to the contrary that she stole him. She merely *found* him.

The Inquisitor, though—she had never seen him before. But his identity was not lost on Uncle Iósaf.

"Huh," he grunted, stepping in front of his family. "Now, what brings the High Inquisitor himself out all this way?"

Ailís raised her brow with surprise. The High Inquisitor? Him? She had seen a man sleeping in a ditch a couple weeks prior who looked quite similar to him, but not once did it occur to her that it could have been the High Inquisitor himself.

"An interesting question," the High Inquisitor said, the breeze from the ocean doing very little to his grease-soaked hair. "Given that you, yourself, are out all this way, Iósaf."

Iósaf put a hand to his chest. "Aww, you remember me? I'm touched, Dónal."

"Some faces are hard to forget."

"I'll say," the merchant added.

At the sound of his voice, Áine began to growl.

"After all," he continued, "how could I forget the face of *you*, girl?" He pointed at Ailís. "You, who stripped me of everything when you stole those eggs from me?"

On cue, Pilib popped his head out of the bag and squawked. A rush of emotions flooded through Ailís—chief among them amusement at the merchant's misery. Apparently, Pilib took enjoyment in the misfortune of others. Confusion toward his continued insistence that she rescued an additional dragon egg from him filled her as well.

But before Ailís could respond to him, Áine pushed past her. The woman shot a finger at the merchant, so sharply it could have flown across the gap between them. "And what would *you* know of losing everything, Liam?"

The merchant—Liam—huffed in surprise. "Áine? Oh, hey, long time no see! I didn't see you there."

"You know him?" Ailís asked.

"You know her?" Dónal asked Liam at the same time.

"*Know* him?" Áine barked. "*He's* the one I spoke of. *He's* the one who betrayed the Draconic Priests to the Inquisition!"

"Him?" Ailís gasped, eyes wide.

"You?" Dónal gasped, eyes wide.

"What do you mean, me?" Liam said, flashing a sneer at the High Inquisitor.

"I am just surprised, is all." The High Inquisitor crossed his arms, tutting his lips. "To think, I had been traveling all this time with the hero who revealed the Draconic Priests to us."

"What? It was directly to you that I had spoken all those years ago."

The High Inquisitor snapped his fingers. "*That's* how I recognized you! I thought I just knew you from my hurling league."

"I *am* in your hurling league."

"I know. That's why I said that's the only place I thought I recognized you from."

"Enough!" Áine shouted. She balled her fists until her arms

shook, her face red with anger. "You would hail him as a hero? Him?"

"But of course!" Dónal responded. "To reveal the hermitage of the blasphemous Draconic Priests and ensure the sanctity and purity of our wondrous land of Nóra—I can think of no braver of a servant of the Thrice-Dead Prophet!"

Áine scoffed. "A brave man? Him? No. Do you know *why* he betrayed us? Solely for revenge—for being fired from a *volunteer* position because he couldn't be bothered to show up for it. Honestly, to think a position teaching our histories to children was so unbearable! For this, and this alone, he chose instead to betray our location and become a smuggler! Does *that* bear the resemblance of a paragon of piety to you?"

The High Inquisitor blinked at Áine in silent astonishment. He pointed a mailed finger at her, then at Liam, back and forth and back and forth, until finally, he looked at Liam and said, "How can she say ~~smuggler~~ legitimate trader, yet I cannot—see, again!"

"*That's* what you wish to harp on?" Liam asked. "Forget about that! They have a dragon with them! Right there!"

A rush of air filled Ailís's arms as she drew her bag open, beckoning Pilib to fully emerge. The dragon seemed all too eager to oblige, baring his small fangs with what passed for a growl. As Ailís balled her hand into a fist, she took a half-step forward, ready to strike.

But she was stopped by Áine's extended arm, her hand holding Ailís back. The woman shook her head, but her gaze did not leave the two new arrivals. "How hideous it is that you consider a young girl more of a criminal than a man smuggling illicit goods to the highest bidder. You are seeking to punish Ailís for mere happenstance, while this man—" She pointed her finger at Liam. "—so readily confessed his crimes in view of you, High Inquisitor. Have you no honor at all?"

"Or brains for that matter," Ma and Iósaf said simultaneously. Iósaf opened his mouth with amusement and pointed at his sister but was met only with a roll of the eyes.

"Funny thing about laws, though, Áine," Liam said with a sneer. "When they are enforced to the letter—such is the Inquisition's insistence—there is little that can be done when you are not presently in violation of anything. I am not in possession of anything which violates the laws enforced by the High Inquisitor. So far as I can tell, the only one doing so..." He extended a hand toward Ailís. "...is the girl."

"And what would you do, then?" Áine asked, her nostrils flaring. "Throw her in chains for something that you yourself are responsible for?"

"Yes, quite so! And then I shall go about my way while the Inquisition is otherwise preoccupied, as I have always done since that day all those years ago."

"Hey!" Dónal exclaimed, putting his hands on his hips. "I'm right here, you know."

"Does conspiracy to commit crimes fall under Inquisition jurisdiction?"

The High Inquisitor hung his head low. "No," he said into the ground.

Liam flashed his teeth in a grin and extended his arms out at his side. "You see, Áine. The Inquisition can scarcely do a thing. Their jurisdiction falls too short every time." He patted Dónal on his shoulder.

"But what of regional jurisdiction, boy?!" A resounding voice echoed through the valley—one that was out of breath and out of patience.

Iósaf buried his face in his hands. "Oh, no. Not this again."

His face red and covered with sweat, Lord Saibhir rushed out from around the corner. Breath was puffing out from his mouth in rapid, ragged bursts as he leaned over, resting his hands on his knees. It was not lost on Ailís that his lavish attire was gone, replaced only with stained smallclothes that had twigs and leaves jutting out from it.

"So much for being rid of him," Ma muttered.

"I'm impressed that he got here so quickly," Iósaf added.

"I should have thrown him farther," Ailís lamented. Pilib looked at her and nodded in agreement. His face, though, seemed to say less, "I'll do more to help next time," and more, "Yeah, you should have." It appeared the hatchling was becoming hangry.

Fury flared in Saibhir's eyes as he pointed an accusatory finger at Liam and Dónal. "You both left me for dead!"

"For dead?" Liam scoffed. "You were ten feet off the ground."

Dónal crossed his arms. "Could not one from your coterie assist you? I see they are not with you now."

Saibhir gestured to his smallclothes. "What marvelous eyes you have, High Inquisitor! Perhaps you would do well not to consort with thieves as I did with brigands!"

With a shake of the head, Liam said, "A fault all your own, but do not lump me in with that sort. The only thief here is that girl!" He pointed at Ailís again. "My trade is one of—"

"It is of theft!" Saibhir interjected. "Theft begets theft, and once I am through with you, I shall take what is mine from the girl! Hide behind the Inquisition's lack of jurisdiction all you wish, churl, but you cannot escape the laws of mine own!"

"If it is my jurisdiction you wish to attack," Dónal said, annoyance filling his voice, "then perhaps we should stress that regional laws extend only to crimes of a human nature. They do not extend to the draconic sort." He pointed his thumb at his own chest. "Only the Inquisition oversees matters of a draconic nature."

"Aye, and what a *grand* job you've done! How many arrests in the last two decades? Only one? *Him?*" Saibhir pointed at Liam.

Liam growled. "If we wish to be pedantic about the nature of laws, should we not examine *your* crimes? Conspiracy to harbor draconic contraband? Possession of illicit materials?"

"I only write the laws! They do not apply to me!"

"Then what of enforcement of false laws? False imprisonment!"

"Those return to a matter of a draconic sort! Why couldn't *you*—" Saibhir shot another finger at the High Inquisitor. "—keep him detained, fool?!"

"Our jurisdiction does not permit—"

"Your jurisdiction permits quite little!"

"But *your* crimes—"

"I commit no such—"

"Draconic matters—"

"Big problem—"

"Dragons! Dragons!"

It devolved further into...whatever this was becoming. No longer was attention placed upon the family and Pilib by the trio of dragon-seekers—they were focused squarely on one another, seeming to remain oblivious to all else as they accused one another of incompetence, petty grievances, and impotence.

Ailís leaned close to her ma. "Can we go now?"

With a chuckle, Ma took Ailís and Camaráin by the shoulders and pushed them toward the Highland wall. "Gladly."

Before she turned, Áine spared one last glance at the merchant. Shaking her head, she muttered something under her breath inaudible over the nonsensical argument.

The arguments echoed as they drew nearer to the wall, and Áine studied its length in search of...something. She had said she'd know it when she'd see it, but that was of little help to the rest of them.

Ailís took it upon herself to search for...something along the base of the wall, and took Camaráin with her. There wasn't much to look at beyond jagged crag formations reaching skyward, the earth dragons' work cresting up in an almost unnatural manner. All Ailís saw was rocks and rocks and more rocks, and it was hardly for her to know what marker a Draconic Priest would be looking for. She was ready to give up and return to the rest of the group.

"Hey, right there," Camaráin said, pointing to some sort of inscription at the base of the wall, where the Cliffs greeted the sea.

Craning her head in the direction of his finger, she glanced at the inscription, a sense of familiarity hitting her. "Doesn't that look like...?"

Camaráin nodded. "The inscription on Uncle Iósaf's library door?"

Her eyes went wide with excitement, and she turned to the

adults and shouted, "Hey! Áine! Over here!" She couldn't be certain it was much of anything, but it was better than nothing. And it couldn't have been a coincidence.

As the adults congregated around them to inspect the point of Ailís and Camaráin's curiosity, Uncle Iósaf huffed a surprised breath. "Huh. Adhamh etched that into the library door long before I moved there."

Áine gasped. "This is it! The marker!"

"Wait, really?" Iósaf appeared aghast. "The Priests let *that* be their guide to the Highlands?"

"Why? What's it say?" Ailís asked.

Iósaf shuddered. "Believe me, even *I'm* horrified by it. It's not for your ears, kiddo."

Before Ailís could press further, Áine put her hand against the marker and drew a deep breath, an unknown word escaping her lips.

The next time Ailís blinked, bright blue skies greeted her.

And dragons. A whole mess of dragons.

Chapter Twenty-Seven

When she took her first steps in the Draconic Highlands, Ailís couldn't believe her eyes. The sun shone overhead, bathing the rich green grass below in an ethereal light. The pristine moors stretched as far as her eyes would take her, unmarred by the hands of man, and were flanked by large stone enclaves on one side that appeared unnaturally carved by master craftsmen and a tall, dense forest of mighty trees on the other. There was even an enormous wooden structure that looked like it could have been a meeting hall. She could hear the sea's waves crashing against the base of the Cliffs of Ard, and ocean spray traveled high enough for small rainbows to be cast in the sunlight. She was stunned to silence.

Growing up, Ailís had walked in on her ma at inopportune times. Sometimes while she was half-dressed, other times while she was sneaking a bite of the dessert she had instructed Ailís not to eat, other times shouting at the neighbors for playing their tin whistles at four in the morning. Whenever those occasions arose, Ma would often freeze mid-stride, mouth half-agape, food sometimes trickling out of her mouth if she had sampled the dessert she forbade Ailís from eating. An unexpected arrival would draw the strangest reactions.

And as Ailís gazed upon the Draconic Highlands, she couldn't be certain who or what drew the strangest reactions.

A host of dragons, with scales a variety of colors and serpentine bodies standing taller than most of the houses in Baile, eyed the new arrivals with suspicion. Some stopped mid-stride to look at Ailís and her family, others had half-chewed food falling out of their agape mouths, and others were carrying lumber on their backs that inevitably fell to the ground. Meanwhile, the newly-arrived humans froze in place like they had never seen a full-grown dragon before. At least the latter was understandable.

"Um...Áine?" Iósaf whispered. "We're not gonna be..." He paused, then extended his arms out in front of him and clapped them together as though his fingers were mighty jaws. "...are we?"

Ailís tensed at the implication. She looked at Pilib, whose silver-scaled head squawked from her bag. "You wouldn't do that to me, would you?"

The trill in the back of the dragon's throat seemed to imply he had to think about it.

She shoved his head back in the bag.

With a deep breath, the former Draconic Priest waved them forward. "We have nothing to fear. Or, I hope, anyway."

The dragons seemed miles away when the family first set out. Ailís thought she'd have ample time to rethink all her life choices that had led her to this moment and whether the moment would end in the belly of a beast she had, until just a few days ago, believed to have no longer existed.

But all the time in the world meant nothing when the dragons encircled them like a pack of wolves descending upon their quarry.

"How's that hope working out for you, Áine?" Ma whispered. She clutched Ailís and Camaráin close, turning their faces into her belly.

Ailís turned her head, flabbergasted at the size of the dragons Never had she felt so small and insignificant as she was when she couldn't even make out the details of the faces looming over her—only the massive scales colored in reds and blues and golds and silvers. At least she got to experience the open sky overhead one more time.

A gold-scaled dragon stepped forward, the earth trembling underneath his massive feet. "Who are you? How did you get past the fae barrier?"

The suddenness of the voice was enough for Ailís's heart to stop for a moment. "They can *speak*?" she hissed. She opened her bag and stared at Pilib, ever the cheerful face. "What *have* you been saying about me?"

A chuckle escaped Áine's lips. Despite it all, she seemed ...calm. "My name is Áine, and I am the last of the Draconic Priests." She half-turned and extended an arm toward Ailís. "I present to you the first Bonded One in generations. I wish to introduce her to the loremasters posthaste."

"A *Bonded One*?" The gold dragon's head lowered to ground level and stared at Ailís, its eyes larger than anything Ailís could describe. "This girl?"

Her teeth chattered from the nerves, but Ailís summoned the courage to smile (such that she could) and stammered out a hesitant, "H-hello." She waved at the dragon for good measure. It paid to be polite.

The gold dragon grumbled, an act matched by the others

with him. He turned his head back to Áine. "Are we to take you at your word? It was not long ago another came to our lands under the guise of a 'Priest.'"

"And I have a strong inkling who you mean." Áine grimaced, spitting on the ground. "Were our order still alive, we would not consider him among our number."

"Strong words. But to my ears, they are just that: words. Have you *proof* of your claim, human?"

Áine turned toward Ailís again and nodded. "Go on, Ailís. Show him."

In all her dreams revolving around meeting dragons, Ailís never once had to think about what it would mean to *speak* with one. More often than not, her dreams would skip that part and fast-forward to the scenes where she was gliding atop the back of one without a thing to tie her down. She clenched her eyes shut, hoping when she opened them again, she'd be atop the gold dragon's back.

Much to her dismay, she was not. Her hands shook, but her ears were graced with words of soft encouragement from her ma, from Camaráin, from Uncle Iósaf, that even as she struggled to open her bag, she felt a strength, a newfound courage. She reached in, her palms meeting with the cold and coarse scales of her dragon's body. Pilib turned over and placed a claw on Ailís's hand, quelling the tremors. A warmth filled her, and when she peered inside the bag, Pilib met her gaze, opening his mouth in an approximated smile. She could feel his reassurance flowing into her, but it was the physical act that encouraged her the most, that no matter what, so long as this little pie enthusiast was by her side, the consequences of this journey were going to be worth it.

And if worse came to worse, at least it would end quickly in a dragon's jaws.

Pilib squawked and trilled as he was lifted out of the bag and presented to the gold dragon. The hatchling spread his wings wide, his small legs flailing as though in search of purchase.

The dragon's eyes went wide, its nostrils flaring. "It cannot be!"

Ailís's arms shook both from her apprehension and Pilib's weight, and she let him down to the soft ground. "He hatched just a few days ago after I rescued him from a smuggler. He likes pies and tarts and sleeping and—"

"Fetch the Great One!" the gold dragon said to his nearest companion, a smaller beast with ruby scales. "He must be informed at once—his son has returned!"

The red dragon nodded and took flight in the direction of the large wooden structure.

"His *son?*" Ailís repeated. "You mean he was—"

"Did you say, 'the Great One?'" Áine asked, clutching her hand to her chest. "You don't mean—"

The gold dragon nodded. "He has been quite cross these since the child was taken from him. He will be...relieved."

A quake sundered the earth, the encirclement of dragons opened, and enormous, dark wings stretched out from behind the wooden building. A living mountain suddenly rose, a heavy groan following it, and without warning, the mountain leaped into the air, landing dangerously close to them all with a mighty shockwave.

"Well...relief may have been underselling it."

Ailís went stiff as a board. With what meager strength she could manage, she waved her arms around her, hoping to find

Ma or Uncle Iósaf or anyone nearby to provide her safety. She felt herself in a void—one where her family had let quite possibly the largest dragon to ever exist land in front of her to do what it would, while they pointed and laughed at her and ran off to who-knows-where. At least, that's what it felt like the longer she stared into the lightless eyes bearing down upon her, its mighty maw revealing a glistening row of teeth the length of swords. Its long, coiling body was lined with scales of the blackest coal. If *this* was the dragon upon whom the Inquisition based its draconic fear, she would understand completely.

And yet when it opened its mouth...that went away.

"My boy!" The Great One spoke with a soft tone that immediately beguiled his gargantuan size. From the stories of him devouring the First Inquisitor, Ailís had expected his voice to be filled with fire and fury, not mirth and excitement. His voice was prim and proper—far more so than anyone Ailís had ever hear speak, and without the uppity snootiness carried by Lord Saibhir. Instead, this...behemoth of a dragon, with naught but two words, assuaged any and all lingering apprehensions Ailís had within her. He stomped forward, resting his head in front of Pilib, his eyes flaring with what appeared to be genuine joy. "Gaotheron! My dear, sweet Gaotheron! You've returned to me!"

"Gaotheron?" Ailís repeated. She looked at the ground, to where Pilib cozied up to the enormous dragon's maw with equivalent happiness of his own. "I still like Pilib better."

The ruby-scaled dragon landed some moments later, huffing and puffing a series of exhausted breaths. "Great One, you did not give me the chance to explain—oh, you've already worked it out, haven't you?"

When Ailís finally looked behind her, she was relieved to see that her family hadn't decided to turn tail and run after all—they had largely frozen in place as well. Ma and Camaráin's faces were a shade paler than usual, and Uncle Iósaf's trousers had become a shade darker, but everyone was otherwise well and present.

And as for Áine—she was stilled not with fright, but with astonishment.

"Great One," the gold dragon said, inclining his head toward Ailís. "This girl rescued Gaotheron from a smuggler—and later bonded with him."

The Great One did not redirect his attention, instead remaining focused on Pilib. "Did she, now?" he said. "Then she has my deepest gratitude for returning him to me." He offered Pilib one last nudge and returned to his feet, towering once more over those gathered, twice as tall as the other dragons. "Girl. What is your name?"

Ailís squeaked at the words, but it was immediately apparent no one else was going to answer for her. "Ailís," she managed to say, before quickly adding, "Great One."

"Ailís," the dragon affirmed. He dipped his head low and said, "My name is Ollepheist. I am forever in your debt for returning my son to me. I can see he has been in capable hands. If there is anything you wish of me, all you need do is ask."

The great dragon Ollepheist. She had only heard his name for the first time earlier that day, but already she had felt his impact across history. The unfortunate circumstances surrounding the First Inquisitor, and everything that followed. The banishment of the dragons from Nóra. The rise of the Inquisition and the black market which arose from their presence. There was once a respect for the dragons that had long since vanished from Nóra. If she could but restore it with a single wish, she would have. But instead, she would settle for a single step.

Ailís gulped and turned to her family. Ma gave her a slow nod, tears trickling down her cheeks. Camaráin clutched his bag ever tighter, his sadness evident. Uncle Iósaf took several steps forward, and placed a hand on her shoulder (and though he tried to pretend he was not exuding a strange smell, it could not be hidden). And Áine, the Draconic Priest who had come into her life by happenstance, gestured her arm toward the Great One.

"Go on, Ailís," she said.

Seeming to sense her hesitation, Ma wrapped her arms around her daughter's shoulders and kissed the top of her head. "It's okay, my sweet. We'll be okay. And when the time comes...you'll return to us."

Camaráin gripped her hand and smiled. "It's going to be much quieter without you around." He chuckled. "But it won't be the same without you around, either. I wish I could..." He trailed off, tugging his bag closer. "I know where to find you."

"And I'll be with you every step of the way," Uncle Iósaf added. "You don't have to be scared. Uncle Iósaf's here for you."

"Quite a show of confidence," Áine said with a smirk. "Considering..." She inclined her head to his trousers.

"I was just...overcome! With...excitement? No, no, we can't think that. It...I..." Iósaf threw his hands in the air. "Fine, I get easily startled. Happy?"

They all laughed, save for Iósaf, whose fake laugh could only be described as "pushing through the pain."

Ailís couldn't deny that she was scared. So much had changed in such a short time. But her family was right—she would be okay. Things would just be...different. There would come a day for the dragons of Nóra, should they have wished it. Whatever small part of that she could play, she would welcome it.

"Well, Ailís?" Ollepheist prompted, his soft voice nonetheless booming. "What may I do for you?"

Pilib turned and scampered over to her, perching once again atop her shoulder. He squawked in her ear, nuzzling his cold, scaled face against her head.

She smiled. "I have entered a bond with Pil—er, I mean, with Gaotheron. I would like your permission to train with the loremasters, so my bond with him can remain safe."

Ollepheist did not waste a second. "It shall be done."

Everything else passed in a blur. The explosive cheers at the return of the Bonded Ones, the celebration for the safe rescue and return of the Great One's son, Pilib—or Gaotheron, for those who were so inclined—and, above all else, the final act of the long goodbye.

How long Ailís spent in the arms of her ma, she could not say. And when the time came, and the promises were shared that they would not be apart for long, there was nothing left to do but the leavetaking.

"I will guide them back through the Cliffs of Ard and through the Crann Woods," Áine assured, placing a comforting hand atop her shoulder. "I'll watch over them, just as your uncle will do for you."

Ailís's lip quivered, but she nodded. "Thank you, Áine. For everything."

The woman smiled, and then looked to Iósaf. She kept a distance from him—largely because of the smell, which had only grown worse—and said, "We are about to bear witness to a new generation of Bonded Ones. See that she remains safe."

Iósaf stuttered over his words, as he did, but still wrapped an arm around Ailís to show enough confidence. "I will. I'll never abandon her again." He tussled her hair, his fingers catching in the knots of her braid.

"Good." Áine closed her eyes, drawing a breath. "And, once Ailís's training is complete...perhaps there may be another calling for you? The Draconic Priests, perhaps? If you'd like to help me build them back up?"

"Oh," Iósaf gasped. "I, um...well, yes, I would...well, you see..."

"Perfect, we can leave it there. Until then, Iósaf." Her gaze lingered on him, and she turned away.

"Until then."

"Ah!" Áine held up a finger and faced the dragons once more before departing. "I almost forgot. Great Ollepheist, there are three who have pursued us who I imagine are still engaged in debates of their own idiocy. They are just on the other side of the wall, if you wish to deal with them."

The Great One nodded. "Of course. Thank you, Priest." He raised a heavy front foot and stomped on the ground—though none of the shockwaves rent the ground beneath Ailís. The ground crumbled elsewhere, a quake audible in the distance...

And then a pillar of the earth shot into the air, three screaming bodies launching above it and landing elsewhere in the sea. The splashes were heard only briefly as the waves crested against the Cliffs of Ard.

Áine flashed a smile, wider than anything Ailís had seen of her, and she waved at them as she led Ma and Camaráin back to the wall, back to the barrier...and back to the Cliffs of Ard.

Ailís's hand remained raised long after they vanished, her uncle's comforting embrace not leaving her until she was ready. The day was beginning to break. She knew not what to expect, only that things would be...different.

"Bonded One," Ollepheist called with a bow. "We serve at your behest. Whatever we may offer you to make your transition all the more comfortable, please do not hesitate to ask."

Pilib trilled in her ear, and his stomach rumbled. It had been a trying day, after all. Scratching underneath the hatchling's chin, she shrugged her way out of her uncle's grasp, offering him a smile in so doing, and wiped away a tear. This night called for celebration for a number of reasons—but there was one in particular she thought would have been best shared with them all.

"Do you dragons throw birthday parties, by any chance?"

Epilogue

It all was a bit sudden, everything that had happened the last few days. Certainly enough to give him cause to stop and think before he would pull another prank on a passerby back home.

On the long walk back to the Crann Woods, Camaráin could think of little else. It was a tremendous weight upon his shoulders—figuratively and literally. He wondered how much Ma would blame him for everything that happened if she blamed him at all. If there was any blame to be placed.

All he could do was watch it all unfold, unable to speak, unable to do anything. Ailís was always the more impulsive one and he the calm and measured. All that time observing offered him plenty of time for the nerves to grow, but he couldn't allow that anymore. He needed to be brave, for Ma especially. The fire within him needed not be tempered any longer.

For now, though, the best he could do was clutch Ma's hand and never let go, not while Áine led them through the Cliffs and back to the woods, words failing them all. Tears had spoken plenty. Camaráin felt the need to remain strong and dam up his own tears.

The curious fae eyes were of poor company as they traversed the Crann Woods, Áine's cottage looming ahead. Were they aware of everything the family had gone through these last few days? Everything Camaráin had read on the fae indicated they had some degree of emotional understanding—though views differed on whether that understanding was used for good or ill. He was not inclined to trust himself to find out at the moment.

When they reached Áine's home, she stopped and offered a gentle smile. "Do you think you can make it the rest of the way on your own?"

Camaráin frowned. "Are you leaving us, too?"

Áine was quick to shake her head. "Not at all, Cam. I just...need some time to myself after everything that's happened. I'm sure your ma needs the same."

As the Priest glanced at her, Ma nodded. The ghost of a smile was on her lips for the briefest of moments before vanishing just as quickly.

"And besides," Áine added, pointing over her shoulder with her thumb, "I was in the middle of a puzzle, anyway. I'd like to finish it." She shrugged sheepishly. "But I won't be gone for long. We've known each other for so short a while, but I owe your family...so much already. And when the time presents itself—" She raised her eyebrows and nodded her head toward Camaráin.

Or more specifically, to his bag.

Camaráin mirrored her raised brows.

"I would be more than happy to see you again. Until then..." She walked up and sandwiched her hands around Ma's. "Thank you. For everything."

"We owe you our thanks far more than you do yours," Ma

said.

Clutching his bag, Camaráin waved to the woman as she retreated back into her cottage. Áine chanced one last glance at them before firmly shutting the door behind her. Though she had vanished beyond the door, it took a few moments before Camaráin stopped waving. It felt the briefest of hellos for the longest of goodbyes.

Ma placed her hand atop his shoulder and led him away from the cottage. "Come along, Cam. Let's head home."

With a nod, Camaráin retook his hold of his ma's hand and followed her. Their path took them past Uncle Iósaf's abode—still a few trees up the road from Áine's—and though they spent only a day there, Camaráin couldn't help but feel a pang of nostalgia for it. He wished he had more time in that library. There were so many questions he wanted answered.

As they passed, Adhamh was lounging on a chaise in the front yard, his hat removed to reveal a balding head framed by strands of long gray hair. Sunglasses blocked his beady eyes, even though there was very little natural sunlight beaming through the dense trees overhead. For as much as he was angry—constantly, frighteningly angry—Camaráin could never have pictured the gnome looking so...content.

"Do you think he knows Uncle Iósaf won't be returning?" Camaráin asked.

Ma scoffed. "I'm sure he's been looking forward to this day for a long time." She waved to the gnome. "Good day, Adhamh."

The gnome's head shot forward with enough force to knock his sunglasses off. His brow crinkled, and there was that rage again. He shook his fists and shouted something at them.

"Nice to see you, too," Ma said, prodding Camaráin along.

"Oh, is that what he said?" Camaráin asked.

"Not even a little bit."

Baile was a sight for sore eyes. Camaráin never thought he would miss the muddy stench of home, but as they say, home is indeed where the heart is. Even if that home always stank to high heaven.

The morning sun was rising as Ma led Camaráin through the village square. As the soft earth squished underfoot, Camaráin could hear the faint and rhythmic noise of a crowd in sync. As he and Ma passed the assembly hall where Ailís's dance recital was—what seemed like ages ago already—he spied rigid signs being hoisted up and down in the air.

"What's going on?" he asked.

Ma huffed with confusion.

Atop a wooden crate stood Miss Róisín, Ailís's dance instructor, and before her stood a dense semicircle comprised of what looked to be half the village.

"What do we want?!" Róisín shouted at the crowd, holding up a white sign with the words "NO MORE RANDOM SEARCHES" painted in bold red letters.

"*A MANDATE FOR WRITS OF ARREST AND SEARCHING!*" answered the crowd.

"When do we want it?!"

"*A LONG TIME AGO!*"

"Yes, we *should* have asked for them a long time ago, but the correct answer is now!"

"*NOW!*"

"No, you say it after I—you know what, we'll start from the top."

Ma's mouth hung wide open. "Uh...huh."

Across the way from the protesting crowd, a group of four Inquisitors sat at a picnic table, appearing altogether shamed. The tall Inquisitor—Camaráin remembered his name as Eamon—buried his face in his hands. Another Inquisitor kept repeating that the Inquisition was ruined, while another was praying—quite loudly, at that—for the quick return of the High Inquisitor.

Camaráin glanced up at his ma with amused eyes, but he was met only with a shaking head.

"I'm too tired for this," she said with a sigh. "This looks like a tomorrow thing."

As the calls for change rang out over the village, the sweet sight of home sent relief through Camaráin. He didn't know if he'd ever see it again, but there it still stood. Untouched, just as they had left it. No signs of intrusion by the Inquisition or anyone else. Once he shut the door behind him, the journey was finally over. It was just not the journey he was expecting.

"Ma," he said, stopping her as she walked across the room and hovered around the threshold to her bedroom. "Today, do you think we could—"

Ma raised her hand. "Cam, I'm sorry." Dark circles had gathered underneath her red-cracked eyes, and not for the usual reasons. "I'm tired. I think we should both just rest today, okay? Tomorrow, we can do whatever you'd like."

Though he had looked forward to having his ma to himself for the first time, Camaráin huffed a sigh and nodded, watching her retreat into her bedroom, and shut the door.

He could hear her collapsing onto her bed, a heavy sigh broken by intermittent sobs. This journey had been a lot...for all of them. And there'd be other opportunities for him to be there for his ma. He had to remind himself of that. For now, though, he was happy to follow her instructions and rest. His bed was calling to him...as was something else.

Shutting his bedroom door behind him, Camaráin lifted his bag off his shoulders and gently placed it atop his bed. Having that weight off of him was a huge relief. He had been cautious not to remove it. It had been a while since he looked inside, not since his conversation with Uncle Iósaf at his cottage. He had been assured that the time would come when it would come, and he was quite eager for it.

Gently, he placed his bag on his bed and opened it, and his eyes lit up at the ruby-scaled dragon egg looking back at him, unbroken as the day he rescued it from the smuggler. He stared at it, running a hand along its rough frame. It was warm to the touch. He hummed in thought, wondering what he could have found had he been given more time in his uncle's library.

On the journey north, he often wondered if the smuggler had done something to it to prevent it from hatching. He had been jealous of his sister and how quickly Pilib's—or Gaotheron's—egg hatched for her. And though he was relieved to still have it, he could not help but be disappointed that it had not yet hatched. The last few days had been an incredible journey, and he did not want to accept this as the end.

After staring at the egg for a few moments more, Camaráin sighed and turned toward his door to get a cup of water. He turned the nob, the door creaking...and then he heard a crack.

Raising his brow, he looked back at his bed and closed the door. The egg was rocking in place. His heart thumped faster as he hesitantly walked over. A fracture ran along the top of the egg, and his breath caught in his chest. Unable to take his eyes off it, he watched as the egg continued to rock back and forth, back and forth...until it stopped.

And a shard of the egg broke off.

He smiled. Perhaps the journey wasn't over just yet.

The End

A Message to the Reader

Welcome to the end of the book! I hope you enjoyed reading UPSCALED.

If it's not too much trouble, I would greatly appreciate you leaving a review on Goodreads and/or Amazon. Reviews are important to authors (especially indie authors such as myself) as they enable us to expand our reach and let more people know that our books exist. Even a simple review saying, "I liked it!" is more than enough! And, most importantly, I'm just curious to know what you thought of this book! I hope to see you in the next one.

If you'd like to keep up with everything I'm doing, you can sign up for my monthly newsletter at joseph-john-lee.com.

Thank you,
Joe

Acknowledgements

This was a fun book to write. After finishing the Spellbinders series, I knew I needed something much lighter to dive into, and this was the perfect palate cleanser for me to decompress and hopefully make some people laugh. This was very much an experimental project for me—I've never written anything that could be described as "YA," or "cozy," or "extremely sarcastic the entire way through," so I'm very grateful to those who helped bring this project to life.

First, to my editor, the wonderful Sarah Chorn. It was an absolute joy working with you on this book. You were incredibly enthusiastic and encouraging throughout your edits, and you really helped me bring it to life. The revision process is always stressful for me, but you made it so much better. I'd also like to recognize the great folks at Miblart for the cover art for this book. You perfectly captured how whimsical I wanted to make this.

To Adam and Sammy, I'm always going to throw you two in here. Without the encouragement from you both all those years ago, I wouldn't be several published books into my career. I'm always happy to have you both in my corner to bounce ideas off of, and your excitement for my projects is always extremely encouraging. You were my first fans, and you'll always be my favorite fans.

To my author friends on Discord, you always make this indie journey less lonely and less frightening. João, Sadir, James, Katie, Michael, H.C., Christer, Joe, Luke, Bethany, and Morgan: it's a pleasure navigating these waters with you. We're the Worst Generation, but the absolute Best Authors.

And, last but not least, to my lovely wife, Annie. I am always grateful to you for reasons beyond just this whole writing gig, but I cannot be thankful enough for how much you support me and encourage me in these endeavors. Thank you for letting me lock myself away in the office to scribble away at these weird books (and I mean, hey, if it means you get to sit on the couch and watch Survivor all night, win-win, right?), and thank you for being my rock. You're the best, always.

Joseph John Lee is the fantasy author responsible for unleashing The Spellbinders and the Gunslingers trilogy and The Dragons of Nóra duology, and has been a semifinalist in Mark Lawrence's annual Self-Published Fantasy Blog-Off. A true product of New England, he prefers Dunkin' over Starbucks, sometimes speaks with a Boston accent, and does not say the word "wicked" in casual conversation as much as one may think. He currently lives in Boston with his wife, Annie, and their robot vacuum named Crumb.

9 798986 383392